T0117086

The North Side

Robert Paluszek

iUniverse, Inc.
New York Bloomington

iUniverse books may be ordered through booksellers or by contacting:

iUniverse
1663 Liberty Drive
Bloomington, IN 47403
www.iuniverse.com
1-800-Authors (1-800-288-4677)

Because of the dynamic nature of the Internet, any Web addresses or
links contained in this book may have changed since publication and may
no longer be valid. The views expressed in this work are solely those of
the author and do not necessarily reflect the views of the publisher, and
the publisher hereby disclaims any responsibility for them.

ISBN: 978-1-4401-8687-5 (sc)
ISBN: 978-1-4401-8688-2 (ebook)

Printed in the United States of America

iUniverse rev. date: 02/12/2010

Prologue

There we were in a playground on a hot summer's night on the south side, Adam standing over Jose's body with the gun in his hand. Blood was gushing out of Jose's stomach. Maz, Joey, and I just stared at each other. What was Adam doing with the gun Joey showed us earlier? Why did he shoot Jose? This wasn't supposed to happen. And what were we doing on the south side?

1

People that lived in our neighborhood called the area the north side. The north side was located in Greenpoint, Brooklyn, and covered fourteen blocks north of Broad Street to the south side of Grand Street. Broad Street separated the north side from the south side. The south side, covered ten blocks south of Broad Street, still had a few white Americans living there, however more people of Spanish decent were moving into the neighborhood. The Polish population mainly dominated the north side, with a little Irish and Italian descent living there. Bedford Avenue extended through both the north and south sides. The year was 1954 and that's where I lived, in the north side at 162 Bedford Avenue between North Sixth and North Seventh Streets. 162 Bedford Avenue was a three-story apartment building. I lived with my family on the second level, above the restaurant that was own by my parents, Jacob and Zofie.

My parents came to this country in the 1930s right before the war. My dad spoke mainly Polish with a little broken English. My mom was fluent in English. Jacob was a tall, burly man. When Principal Haywood from

Saint Francis Prep informed him that I skipped school for a day, my dad took a swing at me. I knew he could have hit me harder, but I still flew across the room.

The restaurant was named after my father: Jacob's Place. It was narrow with a long counter that fit eight stools. There was enough room to fit seven tables in the place. The restaurant mainly served American food, along with some Polish delicacies. My favorite dish was the kielbasa over sauerkraut, a little spicy but delicious. My parents put in long hours at the restaurant -- up at 4:00 a.m. to prepare for a 6:00 a.m. opening, and they didn't close the restaurant until 10:00 p.m. They were open seven days a week with a Sunday closing at 3:00 p.m.

At 5:00 on Sunday afternoon my parents took my two sisters Ashley and Courtney to Sunday mass with me. Our Lady of Help was a huge church with seating for around 1000 occupants. It was a beautiful building located on the north side of Broad Street between Bedford and Driggs Avenues. Sometimes the Spanish people crossed over Broad Street to attend our church. They were very religious; however, my parent's hated them attending mass at Our Lady of Help, saying that they should attend church in their own neighborhood. There was no written rule, but it was understood that the Spanish lived on the south side and the Polish, Italian, and Irish lived on the north side.

Every Sunday after mass we walked over to Frank's Pizzeria right down the block on the corner of Broad Street and Bedford Avenue to enjoy a break from the style of food we ate at our restaurant. There I'd met Joey Bets, short for Bettino. Joey was a skinny Italian boy with a hot temper at times. Joey's parents came over from Italy about the same time my parents came over from Poland.

On this particular day, Joey, his little brother Johnny, and the rest of Joey's family were sitting at a table having dinner. When I walked over to say hello to Joey, he grabbed my arm, took me aside, and before he even said hello he ground his teeth and whispered to me, " That stupid spic Juan from the south side fucked with my little brother the other day."

"What happened?" I asked.

"I have no idea why he keeps screwing with him. Johnny said that he kept pushing him around and to tell his brother Joey, that I was messing with him. Maybe Juan and his boys are sending a message that they think they can screw with us anytime. We should get together and see what this asshole wants."

"Where did this happen?"

Joey hissed, "You believe it? The pricks came over to North Second Street. Johnny was picking up a few groceries at Anthony's delicatessen for my mom. It happened right in front of the store. We have to do something, Bobby."

"Listen Joey, we'll look into this later. Stay away from Juan and his boys. And tell Johnny to do the same."

"Yeah, Bobby, sure I will," Joey sneered.

Just to keep Joey calm I told him that we'd discuss the situation in school tomorrow. But I know Joey wouldn't leave the incident alone. I went back to my family and indulged myself with the pepperoni and meatball pizza. It was out of this world.

2

The next day, I woke up about 6:00 in the morning. My mom was preparing breakfast. I loved her pancakes. My dad was already working at the restaurant. Mom said, "Robert, make sure that you walk your sisters to school today."

Ashley was thirteen and Courtney was eleven. After my mom gave us our breakfast, she'd send us on our way to school then go to the restaurant to help my dad. I'd walk my sisters seven blocks to Our Lady of Help Grammar School and then walk back five blocks to Saint Francis Preparatory High School.

Saint Francis Prep was on North Fifth Street between Bedford Avenue and Roebling Avenue. It was early May and I was ending my junior year. I met Joey and Adam Morley in the hallway between Science and English classes. Adam was a handsome, book-smart person, and we sometimes had him do our homework for us. Joey and Adam were the best of friends. One time Joey and Adam were together when Joey stole an expensive watch from Mr. Hanley, the pawnshop owner. When Mr. Hanley caught them leaving the store with the watch, Adam told him that he took the watch and gave it to Joey. Mr. Hanley didn't call the police because he respected Adam, but we knew he'd probably seen Joey take the watch.

"Joey told me about the argument his brother had with Juan the other night," Adam said.

The bell rang for the next class.

"Yeah, Joey took it personally, you know he has a short temper. We'll meet later after school at the pier to discuss it," I told Adam as I started to walk to my class.

English was my hardest subject. My English teacher was Steve Worciek. He was a slim six-foot-tall man in his late twenties who lived on North Tenth Street. I always saw him around the neighborhood. Steve could have played basketball with the best of them, but a knee injury destroyed a promising career. He still had a hell of a jump shot, though.

"What's up, Bobby?" he said as I walked in the class. "I had dinner at your parents' restaurant last week. The pork chops were excellent."

"Yeah, I know but the kielbasa is my favorite," I told him. "Hey, we have to play basketball sometime -- maybe this weekend?"

"Sure, maybe Saturday afternoon," he said. The class started and I was already day dreaming about how I was going to beat Mr. Worciek at basketball.

3

Right after school ended at 3:00 p.m. I went straight to the pier at the end of North Third Street. The blacktopped street began on Kent Avenue and continued about 100 feet to the end by the East River. There were a couple of abandoned buildings on each side. A wooden pier extended about another 100 feet at the end of Kent into the East River. Directly across from the river was midtown Manhattan. North of the pier was the Budweiser factory, which employed many laborers from the neighborhood. The pier was well hidden from the buildings and couldn't be seen from the street.

Joey was already there.

"Did you cut out of school early?" I asked him.

"No, just last period. If you consider that early," Joey smirked.

We could see Adam and Billy Mazalinski approaching the pier. Maz, we liked to call him. I mean, who wanted to go around saying Mazalinski all the time? Maz is a huge man. There were rumors going around that he once pulled an Oldsmobile with a rope between his teeth.

Adam started the conversation. "We can't let Juan and

his boys talk to us like we're pieces of shit. What should we do about it?" This was unlike Adam, who usually never spoke that way. I guess he was agreeing with Joey.

I told him, "We should ignore them for now and if they want to continue screwing with us, we have no other choice but to deal with them."

Maz agreed with me, but Joey and Adam still weren't satisfied.

Adam continued, "I know where this Juan guy lives, maybe we should go over and start screwing with him and see how he likes it."

I tried changing the subject by asking Adam if he wanted to play basketball with Mr. Worciek on Saturday. I knew Adam liked playing basketball. But Joey and Adam kept on repeating on how they wanted to fuck with Juan and his boys.

"I'm getting tired of this shit. It's getting late. I told my dad that I'd help him clean up the restaurant tonight," I said as I walked away.

The restaurant was packed for a weekday. I helped my father cook and started to clean up so we could close the restaurant on time. It was almost 8:00 p.m. when he said, "Bobby, it is getting late, it is time for you to go upstairs take a shower and do your homework. I will finish cleaning up."

4

I was waiting for the school bell to ring. It was 3:00 p.m. on Friday, two days after we talked about Juan. I couldn't wait to meet the boys down at the pier later. On Friday nights we would meet at the pier at 6:00 p.m. I first went home to check in with the family and have a bite to eat. My mother worked at the restaurant on Friday nights because it was always busy. She wanted me to watch my sisters, but I told her that I already made arrangements with my friends to play basketball at McCarey Park. I didn't want to tell her I was going to the pier. After fifteen minutes of pleading with her, she changed her mind. "Go ahead, I'm sure your sisters will be fine. I'll check on them occasionally."

It was ten past six when I stopped at the restaurant to see if I could grab a few cans of beer. My parents were busy cooking and waiting on tables, so I slipped into the back room and took a six-pack of Bud from the refrigerator and put it into my gym bag. Then I looked up and was startled to see Anne Torbinski, the beautiful waitress I was in love with, looking at me sternly. "And what do you think you are doing, Bobby Lapchek?"

I stared back at her blankly.

"Don't sweat it, Bobby, I was a teenager not too long ago."

I stuttered, "Th-thanks, Anne . . . please don't tell my parents."

"Go and have a good time," she smiled. Anne was twenty years old with the greatest body I ever saw on a woman.

I headed out to the pier. It was a warm night for the middle of May. All the boys were already there. They were all drinking shitty Schlitz beer. I asked them where they got the beer. Maz grinned; he was already half drunk. "I had my older brother buy them for me down on North Eighth Street. Old man Slovak who owns the store is sure a dumb Pollack. My brother is only sixteen years old and he never asks him for proof."

I told them I had the better stuff as I pulled out the six-pack of Budweiser.

A couple of hours passed and we were all feeling pretty good when Adam stated, "We are all going down into the south side tonight to fuck with Juan and his boys."

Joey said, "We sure are," as he pulled out a small gun that looked like a .22.

"Asshole, where did you get that gun?" I asked.

"Listen, Pollack, mind your own business. You coming with us or not?"

It was dark when we started to walk towards the south side.

I asked Joey, "Do you know where Juan lives?"

"Yeah, but I heard that he and his friends hang out on Grant and South Tenth Street behind the Tenth Street pool hall."

On the way, we were getting dirty looks from the people on the street -- looks that could kill. When we reached the alley between the pool hall and an abandoned building there were only a few of Juan's boys hanging out. There was no sign of Juan. Joey asked Jose if he had seen Juan. Jose was one of Juan's good friends. Jose stated, "I know you assholes are looking for trouble. If you have a beef with Juan then you have a beef with me."

"Tell your stupid spic buddy to stay away from my little brother!" Joey screamed at Jose.

Jose said, "I'm telling you and your Pollack friends to go back to the north side or I'll shove a kielbasa up your ass."

Joey then pulled out his .22 and pointed it at Jose. "Listen, I mean business and I'm not saying it again."

Maz stepped in and told Joey to put the gun away. Jose, backing down, said,

"Yeah, we can handle this like men and without the gun."

Just as Jose and Joey started to push each other, we heard the sound of police sirens in the background.

Joey told Jose, "This isn't over, and make sure you tell Juan we were here."

We headed back to the north side wondering if the police were heading in our direction. When we crossed Broad Street we all went home without discussing the fight and why Joey had the gun. I then remembered that I had a date with Steve Worciek to play basketball the next afternoon.

5

It was sixty-one degrees on a sunny Saturday. My parents were downstairs opening up the restaurant. My sisters were watching cartoons on the small television in our living room. My mother brought us breakfast from the restaurant. "Where were you last night? I heard you come in about midnight."

"I was at the park playing basketball until dark and then we went over Adam's house to play some cards." My parents thought Adam was the greatest -- a sincere, well-respected boy. I asked her if I could go down to McCarey Park to play basketball this afternoon. "You just played last night, but I guess it will be alright. Just be back by five for dinner."

It was one o'clock when I started to walk down Bedford Avenue towards McCarey Park. I then met Adam on North Eighth Street. He said, "Do you believe what happened last night."

I told him I didn't want to talk about it right then.

McCarey Park was huge. It ran north of North Tenth Street and continued four blocks to Grant Street, and two blocks east of Driggs Avenue, two blocks west of Roebling

Avenue. There were softball fields, baseball fields, and a football field. There were also eight basketball courts.

Steve was already shooting baskets with a couple of other people I did not recognize. He introduced Adam and I to his cousin Paul and his friend Frank. We started to play two on two, because there were five players, one person had to sit out. Steve could sure play basketball. The man never missed a shot. Adam and I looked at each other in amazement.

The games went on for about two hours, and then we all decided to stop due to pure exhaustion. Steve suggested that we go over to the deli for some sodas. Paul and Frank decided to split. Steve began talking about school and how it is important to try and go to college and pursue a professional career.

While we were chugging down some cold sodas, I was a startled at what Steve said next.

"Why do you two guys hang around with Joey Bettino? I've heard rumors about him. The other day a little birdie whispered in my ear that he was carrying a gun to school. I told the principal about it and had him search his locker, but there was no gun found. I know you two are excellent students. I suggest that you stay away from that idiot."

Adam and I finished our sodas, said good-bye to Steve, and headed home.

Afterwards, when Adam and I were walking home I asked him, "Did you mention the gun to Steve?"

"No way man, did you?"

"No."

Adam and I agreed that the only other person that knew about the gun was Maz. Was Maz a rat? Another thought had occurred to me: maybe Steve was right -- although Joey was our best friend maybe we should stay away from him.

6

I t was the end of June, the end of our junior year and one more year to go until college. I started to work longer hours in the restaurant. It meant extra money, but it also allowed me to spend more time with Anne. She asked me what I was going to do that summer.

I told her, "Nothing special, probably work and hang out with my friends."

Just as I mentioned my friends, Joey and Adam walked into the restaurant. We all sat down at the table in the back. We usually took that table so nobody could hear our conversations. Anne walked over and asked Joey and Adam if she could get them anything to eat. I introduced them to Anne.

Anne said, "I have seen your friends before. They've been at the restaurant a few times."

Joey said, "I didn't know your parents hired such beautiful waitresses."

Anne blushed and said, "Thank you, Joey." Joey had some nice qualities despite acting like a tough guy.

When Anne took their orders to the kitchen, Joey

said, "The principal wants me to go to summer school because I am failing three subjects. I am not going."

I told Joey, "You better go. I don't want to see you get left back a year."

Adam added, "I'm going to take some classes during the summer, we could take them together."

Joey looked away, "Yeah sure, Adam."

Anne then brought out the food.

I mentioned that we hadn't gone down to the pier in a while. Adam said we should go tomorrow.

Joey said, "Bobby, you think you could get some of that Budweiser from the restaurant?"

I told him it would be hard since Anne caught me last time but I'd try.

As Joey and Adam were just about to leave, who walked in but Juan and Jose. They sat at the table in the front close to the window. Joey and Adam sat back down. Joey shook his head. "You believe these two? They come over to the north side like it's nothing."

"Don't make a scene," I said. "They're paying customers and have a right to eat here."

"Don't be so righteous, you dumb Pollack. Adam, let's go over there and welcome them to our neighborhood."

Joey and Adam walked over to where Juan and Jose were sitting.

Adam said, "Welcome to the north side, boys."

Joey told Jose, "You should try the kielbasa. It tastes especially good after I take it out of my ass."

Jose practically jumped out of his seat, but Juan told him to sit back down.

"This is like a reunion from the night back in May," Adam said.

"Where were you that night, Juan?" Joey asked.

"I had better things to do with my life than meet with you," Juan glared at Joey. "Jose informs me that you brought a piece to the affair. Can't you fight your battles without a gun? Does this mean I have to get a piece too?"

Anne walked over to the table and asked Juan and Jose, "What will it be, boys?"

Joey said, "My two amigos were just going back to their neighborhood to have some rice and beans."

Juan smiled at Anne. "No, beautiful, I am going to have the potato pierogies and Jose will have the kielbasa with sauerkraut."

I saw Joey stand up and purposely kick Jose's chair. Joey and Adam then gave me a nod and left the restaurant walking up Bedford Avenue. I knew these two were up to no good.

7

I was watching the nightly news when I heard a knock on the door. My sisters and parents were sleeping. It was Maz at the door. He said, "Joey's little brother got beaten up pretty bad last night. The doctor said he has a broken nose and his left eye was so swollen he couldn't see out of it."

I asked Maz how it happened.

"Johnny couldn't talk much but told Joey that he thinks three spics from the south side did it."

"That is probably Joey's version. Were Juan and Jose there?" I asked.

"Johnny doesn't know Juan or Jose, but I bet it they were involved. Joey's at Our Lady of Mercy with Johnny. The cops were asking Johnny questions, but Joey told him not to tell them anything before they showed up."

"That was stupid," I said. I told Maz it was to late to go to the hospital now. I'd be there in the morning.

It was about 8:00 a.m. when I awoke to the smell of pancakes in the kitchen. I quickly ate four of them and told my mother, "I have to visit Joey's little brother at Our Lady of Mercy Hospital. Johnny came down with pneumonia last night."

"I hope he'll be all right. I knew a person who died from pneumonia," my mother said with a concerned voice.

Our Lady of Mercy was one of the biggest hospitals in New York. It was about ten miles from the north side, so I took the number seven-subway line there. Johnny was on the pediatric floor. When I arrived Joey, Maz, and Joey's parents were in the room. I glanced at Johnny and he looked like he was hurting.

"Hello, Bobby," Mr. Bettino said. I could tell he was upset.

"Hello, Mr. Bettino. It's terrible what happened to Johnny."

"Yes I know, but the little runt said that it happened so fast that he didn't see who was attacking him." Mr. Bettino was a thin man who still spoke with an Italian accent. He turned to Johnny. "Your mother and I are leaving now. I have to get back to work, but we will back later. Hope you are feeling better, Johnny."

As soon as they left, Joey started talking about what we were going to do with Juan and Jose.

I said, "You should've left it up to the police. We're not even sure that Juan and Jose are involved."

Joey glared at me. "Who do you think is involved? I'm going to handle it my way, the hell with the police. They probably wouldn't do anything anyway."

Johnny could hardly speak but Joey asked him to describe the attackers. The description that Johnny gave pretty much fit the description of Juan and Jose.

The doctor walked in and told us that we had to leave because Johnny needed his rest. On the train back to the north side we decided we'd meet at the pier later along with Adam.

8

When I got back home my mother asked how Johnny was doing. I told her that he was fine and should be out of the hospital in a couple of days. I had a quick bite to eat and was thinking of what the night would bring. I had a bad feeling about it and was thinking about making up an excuse and not go to the pier, but I felt I had an obligation to my friends.

I went down to the restaurant to try to sneak two six-packs in a bag. It was summer time and it was harder to hide the cans of beer. In the winter I would just put them under my coat. My father just received a new delivery, so I figured he wouldn't realize that two six-packs were missing. It was a Friday night and the restaurant was busy. Anne and the two other waitresses were waiting on tables. I took three six-packs of Bud from the back refrigerator, put them in a bag, and walked quickly out the side door on North Seventh Street.

I made a left onto Kent Avenue from North Sixth Street heading south when I saw my old math teacher, Mr. Douglas. I tried to avoid him but he called out my out name. I started to walk fast. I didn't want to run, to make it look like I was avoiding him. "Bobby, where are you going?" I was about thirty feet from him now. I looked over my right shoulder and still saw him behind me. I figured he wanted to talk to me about how my summer had been. I knew of an alleyway between North Fourth Street and North Third Street; maybe I could lose him there. I didn't want him to see me going to the pier and found out where we hung out. So, I cut through the alleyway, looked behind me, and didn't see any sign of Mr. Douglas. The pier was now a half-block away.

When I got there, Joey and Maz were already drinking their beers. Maz said, "Wow, that is a lot of beer you stole from your dad's restaurant."

"I did not steal it, I just borrowed it," I said.

"Yeah, sure," Maz grinned.

Joey said, "Where the hell is Adam?"

Maz took a long gulp. "I spoke with him a little while ago and he said that he was coming to the pier tonight."

Just then we could see him walking in the distance with another person. When they reached the pier, Joey rushed up to Adam. "Who the hell is this guy?"

"This is my cousin Kevin from Staten Island, he is staying with us for a couple of weeks."

"I don't give a shit if he's your cousin Karen. Why did you bring him here?"

"It would look stupid if I left him home by himself. My parents would start looking for me."

Kevin looked at Joey. "Do you have a problem with that?"

"Whatever," Joey grunted.

We kept on drinking, talking about the next school year and what we were going to do about our futures.

Adam said, "I am thinking about going to college. I want to become a lawyer. My grades are excellent and my parents have some money put aside."

I agreed with Adam, "I would also like to become a lawyer, I know my parents make good money running the restaurant."

Maz said, "I'm hoping to get a football scholarship. Kevin, that's where I seen you before -- don't you play l for New Dorp High on Staten Island?"

"Yes," replied Kevin. "We played you last year. We killed you thirty-seven to fourteen. I scored two touchdowns."

"Yeah, but that won't happen again," Maz said. Maz was an excellent football player; he was all-city the past two years.

Joey was being very quiet. I could tell he was thinking about his little brother.

Three hours later we were feeling no pain but we were running out of beer. "You want to go over to the deli on North Second and Kent?" asked Maz. "I have a drivers license says I'm eighteen. Forged it myself, and it looks pretty damn good --"

Joey interrupted. "I have a better idea, idiot, just go in the back door and steal the beer."

Maz said, "We have to come up with a diversion."

Everyone was quiet when I came up with the perfect plan.

Adam, Kevin, and I went over to where the snacks were. I took two bags of potato chips, walked to the counter, and went into my pockets for the money. I said to Adam, "I ran out of money, you pay." Adam said, "No way, I paid last time." We argued back and forth for a few minutes. I could see Mr. Diaz getting a little annoyed. Now we started to push each other, and Kevin stepped in, trying half-heartedly to break up the fight.

Mr. Diaz said, "Take this outside!" Then he saw from the corner of his eye Joey and Maz stealing the beer from the refrigerator in the rear. He started to run after them. They bolted out the rear door, dropping the beer to the ground. Adam, Kevin, and I ran out the front door. I could see Mr. Diaz running south on Kent towards Grand Street, but he was starting to slow down when he reached South Second Street. Adam, Kevin, and I were now on South Third Street right off the corner of Kent. We saw Joey and Maz running up towards us, but there was no sign of Mr. Diaz.

"I think we lost him," Joey panted.

We all stopped to catch our breaths.

"Well, we can't walk back towards the north side, we aren't sure if Mr. Diaz has called the police," I stated.

Joey smiled. "All right, then we walk south, maybe run into some friends of ours."

We walked south on Kent Avenue, past several Spanish bodegas. It was 11:30 p.m. and a lot of people were still out in the street. Since it was summertime, even the young children were still out. They had barbeques right on the sidewalk in front of their apartment buildings. I guessed this was they way they lived since there was only one park in the south side. The police let them do it because they didn't want the people start a riot. It was a wonder how people slept at night with all the noise going on.

We passed a group hanging out on the corner of

South Seventh and Kent Avenue. All six of them gave us the stare down. I didn't recognize any of them. A tall, skinny kid with a scar on his left cheek stopped us. "What are you assholes doing around here this late? You looking for trouble?"

Adam tells the skinny kid, "No man, we're just passing by, not looking for any trouble."

The skinny kid sneers. "Then be on your way."

We continued to walk south on Kent, when the skinny kid yelled, "No, not that way -- back to where you came from!"

We turned around and started walking back towards the north side. Adam asked Joey, "Did you bring your gun with you? We might run into some trouble tonight."

"Yeah, I have it right here." Joey took the gun out of his waistband and showed it to Adam.

"Let me take a look at it." Adam examined it like he never saw a gun before. "Looks like a real nice piece . . ."

Just then, we were distracted by some noise coming from a playground on South Fifth Street between Bedford and Roebling. We started walking over and saw Juan, Jose, and three other kids hanging out on the park benches. The playground was about half a block long and not well lit. There was nobody else in the park.

Joey rushed over to Juan, pointed his finger at him, and yelled, "Why did you beat my little brother?"

Juan smirked. "Easy, bro, it wasn't me that screwed with your brother. But I heard he did take a nice beating."

Joey and Juan then went at it. We all stood around watching them wrestle each other for about five minutes before we decided to break the fight up. Joey received a nice shiner on his right eye while blood was pouring out of Juan's nose. Juan was staggering around when Jose stepped in and started pushing Adam. They started to fight, and then Jose pulled out a five-inch switchblade from his pocket. He tried to stab Adam with the knife. We watched in shock as Adam pulled Joey's gun from his pants pocket, pointed it at Jose, and pulled the trigger. There was a loud cracking sound that could be heard for miles. Jose fell to the ground. Blood was gushing from the bullet hole in Jose's chest. Nobody said anything. We all looked at each other in disbelief.

Juan's friends then grabbed him while Jose was still on the ground. They helped Juan out of the playground. Juan and his friends headed eastbound on South 4th Street towards Roebling Street.

Joey looked at Adam and simply said, "What the fuck did you do?"

We all looked at each other while Joey took the gun from Adam and put in his waistband. We then ran out of the South 5th playground exit towards Kent. As soon as I reached South 5th and Kent I heard police sirens coming up from Kent Avenue towards me. I didn't see anyone else behind me. We must have gotten separated. I stopped dead in my tracks and watched the police car make a left onto South 5th Street. I watched the police car stop. I turned my head slightly and saw a policeman get out of his car coming towards me. I started to run as fast as I could, not looking behind me to see if the policeman was running after me. I ran north on Kent and turned left onto South 2nd Street. There weren't too many people out on the street now. I was running so fast, hoping that no one saw me. There were no other streets that ran west of Kent Avenue, just the water, but there were a few apartment buildings between Kent Avenue and the water, and I knew some of the backyards and alleyways. I knew that it was not Mr. Douglas following me; this was much more serious. I headed to the alleyways and climbed some fences before I reached Broad Street. I stopped to catch my breath. I started to walk north on Kent Avenue.

As soon as I reach North 4th Street, I heard a voice behind me. "Bobby, are you all right?" I turned and saw that it was Kevin and Adam.

Kevin panted, "We've been following you from the playground. I'm sure glad you know that route."

Adam said, "Did you see Joey and Maz?"

I just looked at him. "Why, Adam? Why?"

"It sort of just happened. I got so angry with Jose, that fuckin' prick . . ."

"Why did you have Joey's gun?"

Adam didn't answer.

Kevin looked worried. "Do you think Jose's dead? Should we go to the police?"

I shook my head. "I don't know, but I guess we'll find out in the morning. I'm going home now and I suggest you two do the same."

We left each other without saying another word. I walked home thinking, *What is going to happen to me now? Are the police at my door? Are we all going down for this?*

9

When I woke up the next morning I heard my mother making breakfast in the kitchen. I thought, so far so good: the police were not at my house not yet anyway. But what was I going to do? Tell my parents about last night, go straight to the police, or say nothing at all. One thing was for sure: I'd have to meet with the guys and talk about what happened.

I walked into the kitchen. My mother asked me, "Where were you last night? I heard on the radio that a boy was shot last night in a playground near South Fifth Street and he passed away this morning at Our Lady of Mercy Hospital."

I could barely breathe. *Jose died this morning. He was still alive last night. We could have helped him; instead we all ran away.*

I answered my mother. "Oh, nowhere . . . we watched television over Adam's house for a little while."

After I finished my breakfast my mother said, "Bobby, your father needs help in the restaurant today; he needs the back room cleaned out."

"I am going down right now," I told her.

As I was cleaning the room out, Maz walked in. "Your father told me you were back here. Listen, I talked to Joey last night. He wants to take the rap for Adam. He says it should have been him who fired the shot. He had the beef with Juan because of his brother, not Adam."

I glared at Maz. "Do you know that Jose died this morning -- not last night? We could of saved his life by not running away. We could all go down for this."

Maz looked at me. "I know, I heard it on the radio this morning. There is nothing we can do now. Joey wants us to meet at McCarey Park -- he thinks the pier is to hot because Diaz saw us around there last night. I'll see you at the park about two o'clock." Maz left out the back door.

I finished cleaning the back room and told my dad that I was going to the park to play basketball. He tells me, "Son, thank you for cleaning, and don't be late for dinner." I start to walk north on Bedford Avenue when I saw Mr. Douglas talking to two men wearing suits in front of their car. I suspected they were plainclothes policemen. I started to walk faster hoping that they wouldn't see me. I was about twenty feet past them when I looked over my shoulder and saw Mr. Douglas pointing at me. I walked faster, not looking back.

When I arrived at the park there was a softball game going on. Adam, Joey, Maz, and Kevin were talking loud and fast in the stands. Joey and Adam were arguing.

Joey was saying, "Adam, it's over with. I decided to take the fall for the shooting. It is my battle with Juan and Jose for what they did to my little brother. It should have been me who fired that shot, not you -- and besides you have a promising career in front of you. I'll take the whole blame for every one."

Adam nervously said, "No Joey, I fired the shot, maybe if I didn't keep the gun this shit wouldn't have happened in the first place."

Joey explained "No I have already talked it over with my dad and we are going to the police tomorrow. This way nobody else will get in trouble."

We all looked at each other nervously. I asked, "Joey, where did you get the gun?"

"I bought it from Tony Russo," Joey said. There were rumors that Tony Russo was linked to the mob; he ran numbers out of his basement. I told Joey that the police would ask where he got the gun.

Joey smiled and said, "I know, I hope they believe me when I tell them I found it in the park."

We all left the park in different directions agreeing not see each other for a while.

On the way home, I bumped into Steve Worciek. He asked, "Why didn't you come down to the court and play some ball?"

"I felt kind of tired today and just hung out near the softball field and watched the game."

Steve grabbed my arm. "I saw you with your friends . . . is everything alright? I heard about the boy that got shot last night. You guys weren't involved with that, were you?"

My hands were shaking. "No way, I worked late at the restaurant last night," I said, hoping Steve wasn't at the restaurant last night. I then quickly said I had to go home to get ready for work tonight.

I walked back home on Roebling Street avoiding

Bedford Avenue, thinking that the police might still be out asking questions.

It was about 4:00 p.m., and I was feeling guilty about Joey taking the fall for all of us. I knew Our Lady of Help held confession at that time, so I decided to walk over there and tell the priest about last night, knowing that he couldn't say anything. There were three confession booths in the church, and two of the booths were occupied. I heard a voice behind me say, "Hi, Bobby." It was Anne Torbinski. "What a good little boy, confessing your sins," Anne smiled.

"I thought you were working tonight," I said, feeling the blood rise in my cheeks.

"Right after confession."

"Okay . . . I guess I'll see you tonight," I said as I walked into the confession booth.

The booth was dark. There was about a thirty-second wait when the window slid open. The priest on the other side whispered a short prayer and said, "You may begin now." The voice had a strong Irish accent; it sure sounded like Father O'Malley.

I told the father that I missed mass for about two months, lied, and stole from my dad.

"What did you steal from your father?"

I hesitated and said, "It was only some beer from his restaurant."

Father O'Malley then told me, "Say five Hail Mary's and three Our Fathers and don't steal from your father again."

I took a deep breath and told him, "My friends and I

did a bad thing last night . . . we were involved in a fight
. . . "

"Is something wrong?"

I couldn't talk about it any more; I left the booth in
a hurry.

When I arrived home I took a shower and walked
downstairs to the restaurant. I realized that Father
O'Malley probably knew about Jose's murder and may
have a good idea that it was I at the confessional. I looked
out the front window and saw the same two undercover
police officers getting into their car. I went over to my
father and asked him if the two men had dinner. "No,
son, they were asking question about the boy that was
shot last night. They asked about your whereabouts. I
told them that you were here working at the restaurant
with me until late last night. Now, do you want to tell me
where you were?"

I nervously told my father, "Like I told Mom this
morning, I was at Adam's all last night. His father recently
bought a television and the whole family was excited
about watching the new shows."

My father pushed me against the wall with his one
hand, "Do you want me to ask Adam's dad?"

I told him, "It's the truth, Father." He finally let me
go.

I went into the kitchen and started cleaning the
dishes. The restaurant was empty except for an elderly
couple finishing their meals. Anne came back and said,
"Bobby, I am glad you go to confession. I see you're a
devoted Catholic like me. What are your plans for the
future?"

Hopefully not spending the rest of my life in jail. "I'd like to go to a college and hopefully become a lawyer. I know my dad has some money saved for my college education."

Anne replied "I would like to get out of this boring neighborhood and get a new start somewhere else."

I told her with a grin, "Yeah, let's -- it sounds like a wonderful idea."

10

I was eating breakfast the next morning when I heard on the radio that the police had a suspect in custody regarding the South Fifth Street shooting. All they said was that he was a seventeen-year-old white male who turned himself into the Ninetieth Precinct that morning. I thought *is Joey going to turn us in too?* We'd agreed that we weren't going to be seen with each other for a while, but I couldn't take the suspense. I had to talk with someone, so I got dressed and walked over to Adam's house.

Adam lived on Bedford about five apartments down from my house. Adam opened the front door. Kevin was with him. He was surprised to see me. He whispered loudly, *"What the hell are you doing here? I thought we weren't going to see each other for a while."*

I said, "I was going crazy, I had to talk to someone. Did you hear Joey turned himself in this morning? Do you think he told them we were there too?"

"I am not sure but I did hear on the radio that Joey is out on bail until his trial starts one month from today," Adam said.

I told Adam, "That means Joey pleaded not guilty." I

went on to tell Adam, "The police were at the restaurant asking my father questions. You think we could get over to Joey's house and talk to him?"

"What are you, crazy?" Adam yelled.

"Kevin, what do you think?" I wanted someone to say yes.

Kevin said, "I think it's a good idea. This way we all could have better idea of what is going on."

Joey lived on the west side of North Third Street between Roebling Street and Bedford Avenue. The Bettinos lived on the first floor of a three-floor apartment building. When we arrived, Joey was the only person home. His parents just left with Johnny.

The first thing that came out of Joey's mouth was, "The three of you don't have to worry, I didn't rat any one out."

I placed my arm around Joey's shoulder. "What *did* you tell the police?"

"I told them that I wanted to meet Jose alone at the park to discuss why he fucked with my brother. I also told him to come alone. When I arrived at the playground Jose was alone. We started to shout at each other. I was telling Jose that it was him that screwed with my brother. He was saying that it wasn't him. We started pushing each other when he pulled out a switchblade knife and I had no choice but to pull out my gun and I shot him. I told the police it was self-defense. I know it is sounds like a bullshit story but it's the only one I could think of."

I then asked him, "Did the police ask you where you got the gun."

"I told the cops that I found the gun by McCarey

Park in a small wooded area across from the baseball field. The police ran the serial number -- the gun came back stolen from a New Jersey cop."

Adam said, "Do you think the police believe we were there?"

Joey sounded frustrated. "No, Adam, I told them that Jose and I were the only two there that night. My lawyer says I have a good case of self-defense because the police found the switchblade at the scene. I pleaded not guilty. However, he told me that I could change my plea to guilty and I would only have to serve a little time. I have a month to think it over. Now I want you guys to go home, my parents will be back shortly. And pretend that this thing never happened -- especially you, Adam."

I told Joey as we were all leaving, "We will always be thinking of you and I will say a prayer for you."

When I returned home I took a shower, put on a fresh set of clothes, and went to Sunday mass with my family. When we arrived at Our Lady of Help, Anne was sitting by herself in the back of the church; we decided to go over and sit with her. I said a prayer for Joey. Father O'Malley was delivering the mass, and when I went up to receive communion he gave me a long stare. At the end of the service, he was standing at the main entrance shaking everyone's hand so I decided to leave through the side door. I told my mother that I would meet them at Frank's Pizzeria.

Frank's was pretty busy after church. I joined my family and Anne who were sitting at the back table. We ordered two pies, one with sausage the other one plain. Anne brought up the subject of Joey being arrested for the shooting of Jose Nunez. I wanted to crawl under a large rock.

My mother said, "I'm shocked. Bobby, you know Joey -- did he mention anything about the shooting?"

"No," I mumbled, "I haven't seen him since."

Nothing was said after that. My father never looked at me, but I knew in the back of his mind he suspected I was there that night. We finished our piazza pies and went home.

11

School was about to start in a week -- our senior year. It had been a month since I had seen Joey. It was the first day of his trial. There wasn't a day I didn't think about Joey and what was going to happen to him. The police never questioned me. I guess Joey kept his word and never told on us.

Adam, Maz, and I took the subway to the courthouse. Not much was said on the ride there, but you could see the guilt all over Adam's face.

There was a long set of stairs that led up to the courthouse doors. Six large round columns extended up about fifty feet by the front entrance. As we walked in the courthouse, Joey was standing in the hallway with his lawyer and father. "Hello, boys, thanks for coming," Mr. Bettino said with a smile.

Joey gave us all a big hug and said hello. He placed his shaking hands on top of his head and told us, "My lawyer, Mr. Sabol, suggests that I plead guilty to the lesser charge of manslaughter. A manslaughter charge does carry a maximum sentence of twenty-five years in New York. He says if we go to trial for the murder charge, I could be spending the rest of my life in jail. My lawyer made a deal with the District Attorney that I would only have to serve ten years, maybe less, based on the motion of self-defense."

I told Joey good luck as we walked into the courtroom. Joey, his lawyer, and his dad went to the front of the courtroom while Adam, Maz, and myself sat in the last row. The courtroom was half filled. I could see the same two undercover cops that were asking questions about us three rows in front of us. The taller, blonde-haired officer gave us a stern glare.

Everyone stood up when the Bailiff announced the arrival of Judge Everett. We all took our seats, but Joey and his lawyer remained standing. Mr. Sabol said, "Your Honor, my client would like to enter a plea of guilty on the charges of manslaughter and criminal possession of a weapon."

Then the Assistant District Attorney stood up. "I would like to address the court, Your Honor."

"Yes, go ahead," said Judge Everett as he was shuffling some papers.

"The People recommend the defendant serves no less than five but no more than ten years for his crimes. The People have to take into account the issue of self-defense."

You could see the stern look on Judge Everett's face. "So you do. Well, the People and the defendant have to realize that our communities cannot accept this kind of behavior. The defendant has to account for his actions. Although the defendant tried to protect himself, he did bring an unauthorized loaded weapon to a discussion with a person he despised and had other arguments with.

Therefore, I am sentencing the defendant to fifteen years at a state correction facility."

The DA's hands were now tied and all he could say was, "Yes, Your Honor."

The courtroom was so quiet you could hear a pin drop. Adam, Maz, and myself all looked at each other blankly. I could see Joey's chin drop. As the court officer led Joey through the back door in handcuffs, he looked back at us with a proud look on his face. I was wondering when would I see Joey again.

We walked out of the courthouse in disbelief knowing that the judge railroaded Joey. No one said a word as we were riding the subway back home. Adam started to cry.

When we walked out of the subway on North Seventh and Bedford Avenue, we were still in disbelief.

Maz said to me, "Your dad's restaurant is closed."

I was confused "That is weird, he usually never closes the restaurant at this time."

We then said good-bye to each other and agreed that we would not see each other until we went back to school next week.

When I walked upstairs, Anne was watching my sisters. I asked her why the restaurant was closed.

"I'm sorry, Bobby, your father had a stroke and is in Our Lady of Mercy Hospital. He's in pretty bad shape. Your mother is with him."

I collapsed on the couch. I felt the whole world was now·on my shoulders.

12

It was 2:00 in the afternoon when my mother came down to the restaurant. "I'll take over now, go upstairs and check on your father."

My father had been confined to a bed since his stroke five years ago. I had to quit school and forfeit college to help my mother work the restaurant. My two sisters were away at college so that left my mother and myself to run the restaurant, but we got by. Anne also worked many long hours.

When I arrived at my parents' room my father was in his bed watching television. He could hardly speak. Our insurance policy didn't cover a home nurse. My parents couldn't afford to pay on their own, so between my mother, Anne, and myself we all tended to my father's needs. I put down the bed rails and walked him to the bathroom. The apartment is much too small for his care. I told my mother that we should start looking for a larger place.

I was just about to go back downstairs when the phone rang. It was Maz. I hadn't talked to the Maz since Joey's trial. I heard he went away to college. He sounded very cheery on the phone. He asked so many questions at once.

"What's up, Bobby? I haven't heard from you in a long time. What have you've been doing? How's your dad doing? How's the restaurant business?"

I told Maz, my dad is confined to a bed that the doctor says he may never walk again. "I am running the restaurant with my mom. It is hard work and long hours but we get by."

Maz went on, "I joined the New York City Police Department a couple of years ago. The department does not pay well but the benefits are good. I am stationed in Midtown -- it is a great place to work."

"What happened? I thought you were going to college."

"I quit halfway through my junior year. I tore up my knee and lost my scholarship."

"That's too bad."

"You want to get together next Saturday and have a few beers down at the new tavern at North Eighth and Bedford?"

I told him, "Sure, right after I close the restaurant."

When I went back downstairs Anne was waiting on eight tables at a time. The other waitress called in sick that day. I told her that I would give her a hand. Charlie was a good cook. He could handle the kitchen by himself. My mother and me hired Charlie after my father had his stroke. We got ourselves a little breather, so Anne and I started to talk about how rude some of the patrons were. Anne smiled coyly. "Are we still going to the movies on Friday night?"

I said, "Sure, I wouldn't miss it for the world."

13

I made sure we I had enough people working at the restaurant for Friday night. The late movie started at 9:30. The year was 1963, and Hitchcock's *The Birds* was playing. I walked over to Anne's apartment around 9:00. She lived in a one-bedroom apartment on North Fifth Street and Driggs Avenue, one block west of Bedford Avenue.

Anne was dressed casually in a blue blouse and jeans.

I told her how nice she looked. "I am going to have to fight off all the men tonight."

Anne just blushed.

We walked north on Bedford Avenue. The theater was on Grant Street past McCary Park. It was the only theater in the neighborhood and only seated about one hundred people.

After the movie, Anne said, "That was pretty frightening! I wonder how they get all those birds to attack."

I told her, "The movie industry now uses trick

photography." I asked her, "Do you want to have some ice cream at the malt shop?"

Anne smiled. "Sure."

The malt shop was located two blocks west of Bedford on Grant Street. Grant was a busy street with many stores and a few apartment buildings scattered in between. Anne ordered a chocolate milkshake and I ordered the sundae with vanilla ice cream.

I asked Anne, "How long do you plan on waiting on tables in the restaurant? Do you plan on doing something else?"

Anne sighed while taking a sip of her milkshake. "Bobby, you know I wouldn't leave you and your mother with Jacob in that condition. I know it's hard for just the two of you to attend to his needs."

Just then I knew I was falling in love with Anne.

I walked her home after the malt shop and asked her, "Can I give you a kiss good-night?" Anne and I kissed for a couple of minutes before I said, "I'll see you tomorrow morning."

14

The restaurant was busy for a Saturday. Anne and I talked about what a wonderful time we had last night. I said we should do it again in a couple of weeks. Then I told her that I was going to meet Maz around nine o'clock at the North Eighth Street Inn. I asked her if she wanted to come.

"Go ahead, Bobby, I'll close the restaurant tonight."

We usually stayed open till about eleven o'clock on a Saturday night, but we'd been closing a little earlier because some of the customers had been going over to the new place to have a few beers and a bite to eat.

The North Eighth Street Inn was a nice cozy place. A jukebox in the back was playing music from the new British band called the Beatles. There was a pool table in the back with a couple of tables and chairs, and there were three booths against the left wall. The bar was on the right side, about thirty feet long with bar stools. The Inn served mostly hamburgers and sandwiches.

There was Maz, playing pool with another person. He rushed over and we hugged each other.

"Bobby, I really missed you! Looks like you haven't changed. This is my partner in the NYPD, Thomas O'Hara. Tom lives out in Queens."

"Glad to meet you, Tom, any friend of Maz is a friend of mine."

"Let me grab you guys a round of beer," Tom said as he walked towards the bar.

"I see changes in the neighborhood, Bobby, some new business are starting to come in."

"Yeah, I know the restaurant is losing a lot of customers to this bar and the other restaurant that opened up on Driggs Avenue. I'm thinking of getting out of the restaurant business and buying the grocery store across the street. It seems like a better move."

Maz agreed. "Times are changing, it's not like the old days."

Tom had six beers in his hands. "Drink up fellows," he said as he almost spilled them on me.

"The 'job,' as we like to call the police department, is not too bad, Bobby," Maz said, glancing at Tom.

Tom nodded. "We have some fun, but sometimes it does get serious. Let me tell what happened just the other night. We were riding in the patrol car, and we came upon a male staggering out of the Holland Hotel on 42nd Street between Ninth and Eighth Avenues. It's a new project the city is trying to start where people can apply for low-income housing. This man was bleeding from his stomach. We didn't know if he was shot or stabbed. I call for a bus, which is an ambulance, on my radio and Maz calls for backup. As the ambulance arrives Maz asks me if I wanted to go in without waiting for backup. There may be a man with a gun or knife inside that could hurt someone else. Maz went in first as he headed for the front staircase. I walked up the back stairs. We wanted to avoid the elevators. We kept in communication with each other with our radios and took one floor at time. I told Maz on the radio that I heard screaming on the fifth floor. When I reached the fifth floor there was a man walking around talking to himself with a shotgun in his hand. His shirt was full of blood. I then heard footsteps behind me. I slowly turn my head slightly without losing sight of the man and see it was Bryan Howser and Eric Edwards. Bryan and Eric are two other officers that Maz and I worked with many times. I could see Maz approaching the man from across the hallway. The man is short with a stocky built. Maz has his gun pointed at him and I hear him yelling at the man to put the shotgun down. Bryan, Eric, and I start approaching the man from our positions with our guns drawn. The department issues a lousy Smith and Wesson six shot revolver. We are now about twenty feet from the man. Maz is on one side of him with the three of us on the other side. I am now pleading with the man to put the shotgun down. He is just standing there with his head down talking to himself with the shotgun pointed at the ground. It has now been about ten minutes since the incident has occurred. My Sergeant arrives with two more officers. They are now positioned with Maz. The man doesn't stand a chance of hurting anyone else with three of us on each side of him. The man now starts to pick up his head, and seeing that he is totally outnumbered he decides to place the shotgun down on the floor. Everyone rushes to him. I take my handcuffs out and put them on his wrists without a struggle from the man. We escort him down into an ambulance. Sergeant Reilly orders Maz and I to go with the man to Bellevue Hospital Psychiatric Ward and for one of us to take the collar. Collar was another name for arrest. Before we leave Sergeant Reilly rips into us for not waiting for our backup, and with the other breath he tells us what a great job we did. That's what you get sometimes in the NYPD. A compliment and a ripping at the same time. Maz made about twenty hours overtime on the collar and I made about ten. When you make an arrest it takes a while to process your paperwork and then you have to travel downtown to speak with an Assistant District Attorney. The Assistant District Attorney then draws the case up. If the system is backed up then the process can take a while, maybe even the whole day. There are so many cops trying to make overtime, there is not enough room for everyone so some cops sleep right on the floor. But that is an other story for an other time."

"You see, Bobby, I told you the job was interesting," Maz said.

"What areas does your precinct cover?"

Maz said, "The precinct is called Midtown South and covers from north of West 29th Street to South of West 45th Street and from east of Ninth Avenue to west of Lexington Avenue. It is a small geographical precinct but is busy with tourists and commuters going to work. The Port Authority, Grand Central Station, Times Square, and Madison Square Garden are some of the famous areas located in the precinct. The precinct itself is actually on West 35 Street between Eighth and Ninth Avenues.

"Maybe I'll look into the department," I said hesitantly.

We started to talk about old times. Tom was now just

sitting and staring into space. Maz said, "I got a letter from Adam a couple of days ago."

"How is he doing? I heard he was in law school."

"In his last year down at Georgetown."

"I'll have to give him a call," I said.

It was hard for Maz to ask the next question. "What about Joey? Anyone hear from him? Anyone keep in touch with him?"

"One of my customers told me that Tony Russo goes upstate to Greenville and visits him once a month. His parents rarely go up to visit him."

Maz asks me before he takes a swig of his beer, "Do you know where Greenville is? Let's take a ride up there to visit Joey. My next RDO is Thursday. Can you take time off from the restaurant?"

"Sure, but what's an RDO?"

Maz laughed. "I'm sorry, Bobby, it's police jargon for regular day off."

"Then Thursday it is," I told Maz.

I walked home knowing that both of us were ashamed to visit Joey.

15

Greenville was about three and a half hours from Greenpoint. It was a rainy and dreary Thursday. I was driving my 1960 Chevy Impala, a big comfortable car, but bad on gas. Maz and I talked about old times during the trip.

We were about a half-hour away when Maz asked me, "Do you think this is a good idea to visit Joey? Maybe he is pissed off at us for that night."

"No, Joey is a forgiving man. I don't think he'll hold any grudges for that night. I think he will be glad to see us," I told Maz.

Maz was looking away out the passenger window. "I don't want to talk about that night."

We finally arrived at Greenville. The trip took about four hours in the pouring rain. Greenville was a large correctional facility. The place housed about two thousand prisoners. Many of the prisoners were doing time for serious crimes. The security was very tight. When we walked through the large security gates, three guards greeted us. They told us to empty our pockets and put everything in a bin. We then walked through metal detectors. While being escorted by the guards we must have passed about four or five locked gates. We walked into a large room. There were three other visitors talking to inmates behind glass partitions. We waited about forty-five minutes to see Joey. I don't know what the delay was; maybe the guards were breaking our balls.

Our patience was growing thin when I saw Joey walk through the door with a guard. Joey looked up and smiled while the guard was taking off his handcuffs. I realized the last time I'd seen Joey was when he was being escorted out of the courtroom in handcuffs. Joey looked like he aged in just a short amount of time. He was very thin and was losing his hair.

He walked over to the glass partition. Joey sat down in his chair, and through small holes in the glass, said to us with a smile, "Fellows, it's sure good to see the two of you. How long has it been, about five years?"

"You look the same, Joey," I lied.

"I think you're just being polite, Bobby," Joey replied.

"How is it in here, Joey?" I asked.

Joey shrugged. "The guards treat me pretty good but I have to watch out for the other inmates. They try and steal some of your cigarettes and what money you have. There is this guy in here, Mr. Z that runs the whole show. I had a fight with one of his cohorts. The man wanted my smokes. I busted his nose in three places while he cracked a few ribs of mine. The warden threw me in solitary confinement for a couple of weeks after I spent a week in the hospital. He recommended to the parole board that I spend another three more years here because of the fight. I told Tony Russo about it; he usually visits me once a month. He said he was going to look out for me in here. He says he knows people."

Maz and I looked at each other in astonishment. I practically yelled at Joey, "How many years will that be now?"

Joey said while thinking, "I don't even know. I served five . . . probably another twelve or thirteen. But that's enough about me. Tell me what you two have been doing."

I told Joey that my dad had a stroke and I had to forfeit college to run the restaurant.

Maz unwillingly told Joey, "I became a cop."

I thought Joey was going to fall out of his seat from laughing so hard. "A cop!" he kept repeating.

We talked about old times, but it was funny that no one ever brought up Adam's name or the night of the incident. The guards only gave you a half an hour to visit if you were lucky. We said good-bye to Joey and told him to hang in there.

Maz and I went back to my car and started to drive back to the north side.

Maz said, "Boy, Joey sure has it rough in there."

"Yeah, it seems that he has changed a little. Now he has to serve more time in there."

"It doesn't seem right, a man who took the rap for all of us has to do more time. I feel helpless. I wish there was something I could do for him. Don't you, Bobby?" Maz said, practically crying.

"Yes, Maz, I wish there something that we could do."

16

It had been about eight months since I visited Joey. Anne and I had been dating for a year, and I thought it was time to ask her the big question. I set the date up. We would go to New York City to see a play called *The Fiddler on the Roof.* Later I'd take her back to Greenpoint to have dinner at Peter Logan's Steak House where I would ask her to marry me.

The traffic in the city for a Friday evening was horrendous. There was no parking on the street, so I drove into a parking lot on West 43rd between Broadway and Eighth Avenue and paid the ten dollars for the night. We walked to the Imperial Theatre on Broadway and West 45th Street. Before we entered the theater I see a commotion off the corner of West 45th Street and Eighth Avenue. Surprisingly, it was Maz and Tom wrestling with a black man on the street. After Maz put the man in handcuffs he turned in my direction and said, "Bobby! What the hell are you doing here?"

"I'm taking Anne out to see *The Fiddler On The Roof.*

I didn't realize this was your precinct. Is this what you go through every night?"

Tom said, "We are patrolling the theatre district tonight. This asshole was scalping tickets. He put up a struggle but we managed to take care of him."

Maz said, "We have to bring this guy back to the precinct to process the arrest."

"I guess you're going to get some overtime tonight."

Maz laughed. "You see, Bobby, you're getting the hang of the job. Hey, do you want to go over to the Inn tomorrow?"

"Sure, I'll see you over there at ten," I said.

Anne enjoyed the play. The music was excellent but I thought the play itself was too drawn out. I took the Williamsburg Bridge back to Greenpoint. Peter Logan's Steak House was located near the Williamsburg on the Brooklyn side of the bridge. Peter Logan's had the best steaks in New York City.

Anne and I had a couple of drinks at the bar before our table was ready. On a Friday night you usually had to wait about an hour for a table. I asked the hostess if we could have a table in the back. I knew I was going to be a little nervous.

The main entrée on the menu was the steak. Everyone that went to Peter Logan's always ordered his famous steak. When we finished our dinner, I took out the ring I bought from Harry the jeweler and said, "Anne, we've been dating for about a year now . . ." I started to stutter when I said, "Will -- will you spend the rest of my life with me?"

Anne started to cry. "I would love to, Bobby!"

I was a lot less nervous then. We finished our dinner while we talked about our wedding plans. Anne was hugging and kissing me the whole time on the drive back to the north side.

17

"That is wonderful news, Robert! When is the big day?" Mom said as she gave me a big hug.

"In a few months. We are going to have a small wedding," I told her.

"Did you tell your father?"

"Yes, and he had the biggest smile on his face," I said. "Mom . . . I am thinking of buying the store across the street and selling the restaurant. We are not doing the business we used to. I think I want to go into the grocery business. You could make money in the grocery business. The entire building is for sale. This apartment is too small for dad's needs. Anne and I could live on one floor and you could live on the other, and we could have Ashley and Courtney live on the third floor."

"That sounds great. Your father and I have some money saved. We would be more than happy to lend it to you; and you can use the profit from selling the restaurant."

I told my mother, "I will talk to the real estate agent first thing Monday morning." Although she didn't show any emotion, I think she felt sad when I told her I wanted to sell the restaurant. My parents owned it most of their lives.

The North Eighth Street Inn was packed again. I didn't see Maz so I took a seat at the bar. I ordered my second Budweiser on tap when I felt a pat on my back. It was Maz. "Give me a bottle of Bud," he told the bartender.

We took our beers and sat over at the middle booth next to the wall. I started the conversation by telling Maz, "Anne and I are tying the knot."

"That's great news. I always liked that woman. When's the wedding?"

"In a few months. We're having a small wedding. Will you be my best man?"

"Listen, bro, I wouldn't have it any other way," Maz said as he shook my hand. "How is your dad doing?"

I shook my head. "He still is bedridden and still can't speak very well. The doctor says he probably won't walk any more. My mother and I bathe and feed him all the time. Between working at the restaurant and taking care of him we have little time for anything else." I asked Maz, "How is the job going?"

"Tom and I just got assigned to a foot post in Times Square. Let me tell you, Times Square is a crazy place."

I then asked Maz, What area does Times Square cover?"

"Times Square starts at the east side of Ninth Avenue and covers to the west side of Sixth Avenue, north of West 40th Street to the south side of West 45th Street. The New York Times is on West 43rd Street. The Times has a cafeteria on the 10th floor. They have pretty good food. Al the chef is a great cook."

I then interrupted Maz, "I guess that's why they call it Times Square. I know the New York Times Building was there for quit a while."

Maz went on talking, "There are also a couple of the low-housing apartment buildings that are in Times Square. Like I told you before the Holland Hotel is on West 42nd Street between Eighth and Ninth Avenues and the Times Square Hotel another low-housing apartment building is on West 43rd Street few buildings away from the New York Times. The theatre district is on West 44th and West 45th Street between Eight Avenue and Broadway. That's where I saw you and Anne the other night. There is a little sub station located in the heart of Times Square. Some times we hang out in there. The bosses don't like us staying in there. We call some of them Shoe-Flys because there sole purpose is to follow you around and make sure you are out patrolling the streets. Tom and I got caught by one of them the other day. This captain who was dressed in blue jeans and a casual shirt caught us in the sub station reading the paper. He took our names down and gave us a complainant. Our precinct captain probably will instruct us not to go in the sub-station anymore unless we were assigned there. I know it sounds a little childish but that's the New York City Police Department. Tom and I usually patrol 42nd Street from Eight Avenue to Broadway. On a given night there are about ten officers assigned to that one block. The precinct itself turns out about 50 officers at roll call. Roll Call is where we get our assignments for the day. It usually held at the precinct.

On Forty-Second Street there are mostly pornographic shops and pornographic movie theatres. The pornographic stores mostly sell novelty gimmicks and x-rated movies. There are many drug dealers on the block. They are usually selling pills and cocaine. These drug dealers get collared all the time but these liberal judges let them out the next day. They do a lot of there selling in the movie theaters. There are also a few places fast food places to eat but I wouldn't touch any of the food from these places, there are usually mice running around. There are two gift shops on 42nd street between Eight and Seventh Avenues, one on the south the other on the north side of the street. The gift shop on the north side of 42nd street sells many police items. The owner Mr. Lee is not allowed to sell firearms but he does sell police authorized equipment like flashlights, handcuffs, batons and all different kinds of holsters. In fact some idiots take out their illegal guns in the store to see if the gun fits in the holster. Mr. Lee, a thin, six-foot gentleman of Chinese descent is always willing to work with us. In fact Tom and I would hide across the street from the store and observe people going to Mr. Lee's store. Then we would approach the store and observe through the window. Mr. Lee would signal us by scratching his head if some one was trying to fit their gun into a holster. We would then wait until the person is far away enough from Mr. Lee's store, not to make it look obvious and then stop the person and ask him or her questions. If we observed a bulge on the person's body, we had the right to frisk that person. A few people that we did stop were off-duty police officers or correction officers who were authorized to carry a firearm. Many officers do make many arrests for Criminal Possession of a Firearm but like I told my Sergeant it was so easy that Mr. Lee should be the one given a metal.

The owners of the movie theaters also let us walk through the movie theaters to see if there is any illegal activity being performed. Many people buy cocaine on the street and go inside to take the drug or they would proposition a prostitute inside the theater. It is a great way to have sex because it is so dark in the theater. Last night I got about ten hours overtime by collaring this middle-aged man nicely dressed in a suit and tie for having sex with a prostitute right in the back of the theater while an x-rated movie was playing. The man works on Wall Street. I shined my flashlight on him and caught him right in the act. Usually after we place them under arrest for the prostitution charge they also have some kind of drugs in their pockets so we also hit them with the Criminal Possession Of a Controlled Substance. I did feel sorry for the man; he has a family but what the fuck it meant that I was going to make overtime on him.

There are also about four to six 10-13 radio calls a night. A 10-13-radio signal call is when a police officer needs assistance. Believe me when an officer calls a 10-13 the whole police department shows up.

This is the basic night on 42nd street. The days are not as bad as the nights. We do flip-flops; flip-flops are one week of four by twelve's at night and one week of eight by fours during the day. Bobby, are you still thinking of joining?"

"Maybe? I told Maz. "But my family and I are selling the restaurant and buying the apartment building across the street. I'm thinking of opening a grocery store. There are fewer hours to work and we probably could make more money. Anne and I could live on the first floor with my parents living on the second. My sisters could live on the third floor."

"Wow" Maz said, "that sounds like a plan." Before we had our last drink, Maz said, "Bobby I have a funny story to tell you that happened at the precinct the other day. Dutch, a dinosaur and a prankster, had me in stitches."

"What the hell is a dinosaur?"

"Oh, we call cops who have a lot of time on the job dinosaurs."

Maz went on. "I made a collar for drugs. I brought my perp back to the precinct and put him in the holding cell. My perp was being belligerent. He said that it was a bullshit arrest. That he didn't do anything. He just kept going on and on. So Dutch walks in with a judge's robe on. Believe me, Dutch plays the part well. He has salt-and-pepper hair and looks like a judge. There are three perps in the cell. You could now see that they are getting nervous and being polite to Dutch. Dutch asked my perp, 'What have you been arrested for?' He stutters, 'I only bought a little marijuana.' Dutch then says, 'A little marijuana! That is bullshit. I can't have drug dealers like you on my streets. The state sentences you to three years in prison.' The perp jumps up. 'Three years for buying marijuana. Come on, Judge, please let me go!' I was in hysterics. I walked out of the room and burst out laughing. When I went back in to the holding cell, Dutch told my perp he would see what he could do. 'But you have to be on your best behavior and listen to your arresting officer.' The perp agreed. He was a gentlemen the rest of the night and I didn't hear any more bullshit from him."

I told Maz that was a great story and then we called it a night.

18

It only took two months to sell the restaurant. A Russian family bought it from us at a reasonable price. The transition from moving to the apartment across the street went pretty smoothly. I picked the biggest bedroom on the second floor for my father's hospital bed. Since we no longer had the restaurant and I was opening up the grocery store, my mom didn't have to work anymore. Our new address was 183 Bedford Avenue.

Since Anne and I planned the wedding for the next month, I moved into the first floor by myself. My sisters moved in on the third floor.

The store on the ground floor was small and narrow. There were two aisles with an island that contained groceries in the middle. When you walked in, the cash register was in the front on the left hand side. In the back were three freezers and two refrigerators. There was a long counter in the back were I was going to sell cold cuts and meats. I took Charlie, the cook from the restaurant, to serve the cold cuts and meats. I also hired two delivery boys: Michael Pinski and Joey's younger brother, Johnny. It was the least I could do for Joey. I called it the North

Seventh Street Grocery Store. This way everyone knew where it was. I opened the store seven days a week from 7:00 a.m. to 7:00 p.m., but closed at 2:00 p.m. on Sunday. It was a good location for commuters. There was a bus stop right in front of the store, and just around the corner was the North Seventh and Bedford Avenue subway station.

The first two weeks were pretty busy. Saturday was the busiest day of the week. There were many deliveries on Saturday. I made sure both Michael and Johnny were both working on that day. After I closed the store at seven, I went up to see if my mother needed any help with Jacob. I was exhausted from the busy day at the store. I also had plans to go out to dinner with Anne later in the night. We were going over to Peter Logan's Steak House to talk about the wedding plans. I picked up Anne at 9:00 pm.

"Only two more weeks till the wedding" Anne's mother, Veronica, said.

"Are you excited?" her dad, Anthony, added. Her parents were the sweetest people you would ever meet.

"We are going over to Peter Logan's to finalize the plans. Would you like to come?" I asked.

"Anne's mom just made the greatest potato pierogies. I am stuffed. Thanks anyway."

It was a beautiful August night so we walked over to Peter Logan's. We walked through the south side. The neighborhood was changing. Different ethnic backgrounds were moving into the area. I was wondering if Juan was still living in the south side. There was an hour wait for a table at Peter Logan's. The place was getting more well known. Many famous people and politicians were having dinner here. We talked about the wedding for a while and who was coming.

Anne asked me, "Did you ever get a response from Adam Morley?"

"I sent an invitation to an address that Maz gave me in Washington D.C. but I didn't get a response from him. How many guests do we have coming to the wedding?"

"About fifty. I wanted to keep it small. I have a few friends and some relatives from Staten Island coming."

The ceremony was going to be at Our Lady Of Help, and the reception was being held at the American Polish Hall on Kent Avenue and North Tenth Street.

I told Anne, "Maz and a few friends are taking me over to the city next Saturday for a dinner and a few drinks. I guess it is going to be my last night out as a bachelor."

Anne said hesitantly, "Well . . . have a good time and stay out of trouble."

I walked Anne back home and kissed her goodnight.

19

I met Maz at McMann's Pub on West 34th Street and Eighth Avenue, one block from the Midtown South Precinct. McMann's served some hot food -- roast beef, pastrami, and turkey. It was happy hour. You could buy two beers for the price of one.

"Give me a round for everyone. Dave, this is my best friend, Bobby. The poor soul is getting married in a week," Maz told the bartender.

"Glad to met you, Bobby. Marriage isn't as bad as some people think. I've been married to my wife for twenty-seven years. The first round is on me." Dave was in his fifties with salt-and-pepper hair; he'd been tending bar at McCann's for eighteen years.

Maz brought Tom, Bryan, and Eric with him. "Congratulations, Bobby," Bryan said.

"For what? The man still has a week to change his mind," Maz laughed.

I ordered the hot roast beef with a baked potato and corn. We were on our fifth beer when I asked Eric, "Why are you walking around with a limp?"

Bryan said while chomping on a cheeseburger, "Eric

and I had a stabbing early this morning. It was our first job of the day. We walk up four flights to this apartment building at 356 West Thirty-ninth Street. We discover this man in his early thirties lying in his bed with about twenty knife wounds to his body. There was blood everywhere. The apartment was rundown, with cockroaches walking on floor and even on this poor man's body. This guy was definitely DOA. We don't know how long he has been dead for, so Eric and I start searching the building for the perp.

"Maz and Tom now arrive at the scene. They walked over from Forty-Second Street. Eric says he heard some noise coming from the rear yard. He looks out the back kitchen window and sees this guy who looks at him then takes off running over a fence and into the next yard. I call a ten-thirteen over the radio while Eric climbs down the fire escape by the kitchen window. Eric is more of an athlete. Tom and I take the easier way and run down the stairs. Maz has to stay with the body to preserve the crime scene.

"Tom and I turn left from west Thirty-Ninth Street onto Eight Avenue, heading north. We see Eric about a half a block ahead of us. Eric turns left into the Port Authority Bus Terminal. The Port Authority is full of commuters and visitors from other states. The Port Authority police are usually busy with drug dealers and chasing the homeless into the street -- which then becomes our problem. Eric is now heading into the subway, which is located under the Port Authority. The A and C subway lines run under Eight Avenue. I grab my radio and asked the dispatcher to notify Port Authority police and transit police for help before we went into the subway.

"Tom and I hop over the turnstile and run down the stairs to the northbound A train platform. We are directly under 42nd Street. I look up and down the platform; Eric is nowhere in sight. We start to walk upstairs when we meet a transit officer. He heard over his radio that an officer is chasing a perp towards a tunnel by the Seventh Avenue and West 42nd Street station. There are many tunnels that lead from Eight Avenue to Seventh Avenue from West 41st Street to West 44th Street. It is like a maze down there. As Tom and I arrive at the Seventh Avenue subway we see Eric jump off the platform and run into the tunnel. It's close to rush hour and the trains usually run every ten minutes. There is a blue light every five hundred feet. There is also a switch under the light. This switch stops the train temporally until the radio dispatcher can reach the conductor to inform him about the situation.

"I'm about three hundred feet behind Eric when I see him fall and he's not getting up. I could hear the sound of a train in the distance. I run over to the first blue light I see and pull the switch hoping the sound of the train stops. Only emergency personnel know about the blue light. A few seconds seems like a few hours but I didn't hear the sound of the train anymore. Tom and I were joined by two transit officers as we walked over to see how Eric was doing."

Eric added while finishing his beer, "Yeah. You'd think that prick was running a marathon. My ankle was a little swollen. Bryan took me to the hospital. The doctors took some x-rays but they came out negative. My only regret was not catching him."

Tom picked up the story. "Bryan and Eric went to St. Luke's while I went back to the crime scene. Maz was talking to the detectives when I arrived. They think the incident was a gay lovers' quarrel. The victim and perp were roommates. The detectives usually get their man -- or may I say in this case, woman."

We all looked at each other and laughed.

We started to play darts in the back room. Maz came over to me and said, "Listen, Bobby, Tom and I are thinking of taking you over to the whorehouse up at West 48 Street. We are friendly with the lady who runs the operation. You game?"

I grinned. "Absolutely."

After we finished darts, Bryan and Eric said good-bye and wished me the best, as did Dave the bartender.

Maz, Tom, and I started to walk up Eighth Avenue. There were many low budget electronic stores and small bodegas in the area. The closer we got to 42nd Street, the more porn shops there were. The front windows of the porn stores displayed X-rated movies. We walked into one porn shop. All you could find was a display of hundreds and hundreds of x-rated movies. In the back of the place were these tiny little booths called peep shows. You put a quarter in and an X-rated movie comes on for about five minutes.

Maz said, "I had a sixty-five-year-old man from the Midwest have a heart attack and die right in on of those booths. The guy was about four hundred pounds. It took four of us to help the morgue guys carry him into the meat wagon. It was hard to tell his wife over the phone that her husband had a heart attack and passed away in a porn place. However, I didn't tell her where it happened."

I started to laugh. You could see the anger on Maz's face when he said, "That's the truth, you stupid Pollock."

We left the store and were now on West 42nd Street and Eighth Avenue. I asked, "What's that building with all the neon lights across from the Port Authority?"

Maz says, "That's Porn World, probably the sleaziest porno place in the world. The women participate in the craziest sex acts. They even have sex with animals. I saw one women have sex with a pony. We are not going there."

Just then, three men came up to us and asked if we'd like to buy some drugs from his buddy down the block.

Maz told us, "The drug dealers usually sell LSD and cocaine."

As soon as Maz showed them his badge they bolted towards Seventh Avenue. Maz said, "Those guys are the steerers or lookouts; they don't carry the drugs, just tell you who you can buy them from."

We proceed to walk one more block to West 43rd Street and Eight Avenue.

Maz said, "Tom and I have to go downtown and receive a medal for saving a fellow officer from a fire at the Times Square Hotel over there."

"What happened?" I asked.

"We were patrolling one night when we saw smoke coming from one of the floors above us. We were the first on the scene, so Tom called for help and we went into the building. They teach you at the academy to never run into a burning building. What you should do is call for help and wait for the firemen. Not only did we not wait for the firemen, but also we took the elevators with two emergency medical technicians. You should walk up the stairs and never take an elevator during a fire. Luckily the elevator was still working. We could hear screaming as we approached the eleventh floor. The occupants that lived in the building were mostly low housing rentals. We stopped the elevator on the eleventh floor, which led right into the fire. This was the third mistake we made. But we did stay low to the ground knocking on doors and telling the people to leave. Some of the occupants had to be carried out. This one girl about ten years old fainted right in my arms while I was carrying her. Tom and I carried the occupants down to two floors below the fire then headed back up. The smoke was now getting heavy when I saw a fellow officer, Jimmy Funato, lying on the floor passed out. I called to Tom to grab his feet while I placed my hands under his arms and carried him two flights down. We then handed him to the two same medical technicians. One of the medical technicians placed an oxygen mask over his mouth and in a few seconds Jimmy started to wake up. We then started to walk back up, but by now there were enough firemen around to help everyone. When I walked out of the building an emergency technician grabbed my arm and led into one of the ambulances to get treated. Sergeant Reilly was already in the ambulance being treated. He said, 'Great job! I guess you were as dumb as me to go into the building.' Sergeant Reilly and myself rode in the ambulance to Saint Luke's Hospital to get examined for smoke inhalation. There I met Tom; he arrived in another ambulance."

I laughed. "The brass is going to give you two medals for all the mistakes you made?"

"Don't be a wise ass, Bobby," Tom said.

We finally arrived at the brothel at West 48th and Eighth Avenue. It was an old and run-down, six-story building.

Maz said, "Bobby you're not chickening out, are you?"

"No way," I said as I nervously looked around before entering the building.

"The apartment is located on the ground floor near the rear of the building," Maz said as we followed behind him.

Maz knocked on the door, and a lady's voice called from behind the door, "Who is it?"

"It's your friend William from the precinct."

I was a little startled that Maz told the lady out front that he was a police officer.

The door opened and a little Oriental woman in her mid-forties said, "I haven't seen you in quite a while."

"I've been busy fighting crime, you know how it is. Have you been pinched lately?"

"No, no, business has been good."

Maz turned to us. "Ms. Chau, you know my partner, Tom, and this is my best friend, Bobby. Bobby is getting married next week. You have to take good care of him tonight, maybe give him a special."

Ms. Chau laughed. "Congratulations, Bobby, we will take good care of you."

The apartment had a long and narrow hallway with many little rooms. Most of the doors were closed. I assumed there were customers behind some of the doors.

Ms. Chau led us to a large room. There was a television on and two men sitting on a large brown leather sofa.

There was another man with a shaven head that I would say weighed about 300 pounds standing next to a small bar. I figured he was a bodyguard for Ms. Chau.

I was starting to get a little nervous when Ms. Chau asked us, "Could I get you boys something to drink?"

Maz said, "We will have a beer."

Ms. Chau took out three cans of Pabst Blue Ribbon from the refrigerator behind the bar and handed them to Maz with a smile. I looked at Tom and saw that he was getting a little nervous as he stood up and began to pace.

Maz was talking to a beautiful young Asian woman in the hallway. It seemed to me that he knew her pretty well. Another Asian woman entered the room and walked over to one of the guys sitting on the couch. The man was well dressed and in his late forties. The man grabbed the Asian woman's outstretched arm and they both walked down the hallway into one of the rooms.

Maz was now finished talking to the girl and came over to Tom and myself. "Bobby, I have a special girl for you. She will be out in about ten minutes."

"How special is she?" I asked.

"Oh, she is --"

Suddenly, we heard a loud bang coming from the front door. I jumped out of my seat to see what the hell was going on, and observed that the front door was bent and two of the three locks were practically falling off. There was still one lock holding the door in place.

Tom shouted, "Shit, that must be vice!"

Ms. Chau said, "Quick, come this way -- there is another way out!"

It seemed that she had been through this drill before.

We all followed her down the hallway. Ms. Chau, three Asian women, and the man that was sitting on the couch were before me. Tom and Maz were behind me. Ms. Chau lead us to a door in the back of the apartment. Just as we were almost through the doorway, the front door was slammed open. Tom, Maz, and I looked back and noticed a police officer wearing a wind breaker jacket with the letters N.Y.P.D. written on it and holding up a badge in his right hand. The officer made eye contact with us, but he was mostly looking at Maz. Maz quickly looked away as we ran out the back door.

Ms. Chau told us, "Walk fast but don't run."

She then went back inside. I heard the door lock as we started to walk fast. We were now in a little alleyway that led us onto West 49th Street between Eighth and Seventh Avenues.

"Lets go this way," Maz said as we walked east on West 49th Street towards Seventh Avenue.

Nobody said a word until we reached the corner of Seventh Avenue and West 49th Street. The streets were lit up with all the neon lights. You could see the sweat pouring off Maz's face "Shit, I think that was Lieutenant Mulligan. He was the Lieutenant I had when I worked the Forth of July detail last month. Do you think he recognized me?"

I was honest with Maz. "He sure did stare at you for a while."

"Shit!" Maz yelled. "Well, there's nothing I can do now."

We walked to the Times Square subway station at West 42nd Street and Broadway. Tom shook my hand and Maz gave me a hug. "Sorry your night was cut short, buddy. I guess we'll see you next Saturday on your big day."

I waited about ten minutes before I caught the number seven-train home.

20

Our Lady of Help Church was beautifully decorated for our wedding. Father O'Malley conducted the ceremony. He still looked at me in a disconcerting way but never mentioned the time in the confessional. I wondered if he still thought it was me that talked to him that day.

Anne looked stunning in her wedding dress. The ceremony went beautifully. Anne and I had some pictures taken in front of the church with our families, Maz the best man, and Anne's cousin, Lori, who was the maid of honor. My sisters brought my father in his wheelchair to the church, but he was unable to attend the reception. It was difficult enough for him just to attend the ceremony.

After we took pictures, Anne, Lori, Maz, and I jumped into a limousine and went to the reception at the Polish American Hall. We had a Polish band that played both traditional and contemporary music. There were around fifty people at the reception. About half were family members while the other half were friends.

I invited Tom, Charlie, and Johnny, along with a few friends from the neighborhood.

Maz introduced me to his girlfriend, Janet.

"Nice to meet you, Janet. Maz has only nice words to say about you," which was a little flattery that I added. Maz never mentioned that he had a girlfriend.

Tom came alone. I think he was trying to hit on Lori. They were dancing from the start of the reception.

A few hours later, Maz pulled me aside along with Tom and said, "Bobby, can we talk?" We grabbed a few beers from the bar and went outside. Johnny came along with us.

I asked Johnny, "How is Joey doing? Have you visited him lately?"

Johnny looked me in the eye. "I went up to Greenville two weeks ago. Bobby, he is not doing well. In fact, he seems depressed to me. He says Tony Russo is the only other person that visits him beside myself. I hope he doesn't get involved with him -- I think the grease ball is connected to organized crime."

"Me too," I said. "We have to go up and visit him soon . . . maybe when I get back from my honeymoon."

Maz then looked at me and said, "That asshole lieutenant went and squealed to our captain about the other night."

"What did he say?" I asked.

"The asshole told him that he seen me in the prostitution house while he was performing his operation --"

Tom interrupted. "Captain McGuire had us in his office for about an hour tearing us a new one."

Maz continued. "The captain told us that he came

on the job with Lieutenant Mulligan twenty-one years ago. He said that was a good thing because Mulligan was thinking of going straight to the Internal Affairs Bureau. Then the captain told us he had bad news for us -- that he is transferring us uptown to the 30th Precinct.

I asked Maz, "Where is the 30th Precinct located?"

Maz told me, "The captain said it's on the west side of Harlem and south of Washington Heights. It is the drug capital of the world. It is not such a bad thing the Captain said. You boys can make a lot of overtime there. There are many home invasions there. I then asked him what the hell are home invasions? Home invasions are when the perps go into apartments looking for drugs. If they cannot find the drugs or if the people in the apartment who are drug dealers themselves don't tell them where the drugs are they usually tie the owners up and torture them by stabbing or even shooting them. It would be a good day if they let them live. The owners hide the drugs in traps. It's usually hard to find theses traps. They are well hidden. When a warrant is issued to search the place we find the traps under bathtubs or even in floor joints. I told the Captain in a sarcastic voice wow that sounds great. I asked him why is he transferring us to Harlem. Nothing happened that night. Mulligan was the only person that seen us. The incident never got out. I also told him that the madam told me (not to mention names) that there were a few high ranking officials that visit the apartment on a regular basis. Captain McGuire said I'm sorry boys but I have to cover your asses as well as mine just in case Mulligan did go to the Internal Affairs Bureau. He further stated that you did not want to open a can of worms by mentioning high-ranking officials. He did give us a word of advice by saying there's a lot of drug money going around in the 30th precinct. Don't be tempted to take any. It is not worth losing your job or doing time. I thanked him for the advice. So next week Tom and I are going to Harlem."

I told Maz and Tom, "Hey, I'm sorry that we went up there that night."

Tom said with a smile, "It was our idea. Don't worry and enjoy the rest of your night."

We went back inside. Maz, Tom, and Johnny went straight to the bar for another drink. I joined Anne. It was time to cut the cake. After we all had cake it was time for Anne to throw the bouquet and for me to toss the garter. It was ironic that Lori caught the flowers and Tom caught the garter. Maybe there was some kind of inside help. Tom used an old trick of hiding a pair of lady's underwear in his hand while placing the garter on Lori's leg. He went up far enough to make it look like he pulled down the underwear Lori was wearing. Everyone enjoyed the gag. It was the near the end of the wedding when Anne and I were carried out on Maz and Tom's shoulders. We waved good-bye as the limousine drove us away.

21

It was three o'clock in the morning. Barbara was crying in the nursery. It was my turn to feed her. Barbara was getting her first tooth. Anne was pregnant with our third child. Jack, our first child, was three years old. Jack awoke from Barbara's crying. I told him, "Go back to sleep, little one." Jack slept in his crib with us in our room. We only had two bedrooms in the apartment, so it was a little tight. I told Anne that we'd have to start looking for a new place, maybe a house of our own.

My dad was still bedridden. I was hoping to get another place close to him. Anne's Father had passed away a couple of years ago. He had a construction accident. Anne took his passing very hard. Her mom lived alone, and when we buy our first home, hopefully she could live with us.

It took me about five minutes to warm up the milk. I sat down in my comfortable chair and fed Barbara. I then went back to bed for a couple of hours. I had to open the store at seven o'clock.

The grocery store business was doing pretty well. I made most of my money on deliveries. Charlie was still the man cutting cold cuts. Johnny left for a bartending job at the North Eighth Street Inn. It had been five years since I had visited Joey at the Greenville Correction Facility. I had been too busy with the family and the store.

Maz called me the other day. He wanted to get together to have a few beers. We kept in touch every now and then.

David, the guy who I bought my cold cuts from, entered the store. "Bob, I have three salamis, two roast beefs, three bolognas, and six turkey breasts for you."

"Sounds good to me."

"What's cooking?" David asks while handing me the bill.

"Holy shit!" I nearly fainted when I looked at the bill. "Your prices went sky high."

"I have to make a living too," David said with a smile. "How is the family doing?"

"They're all doing fine. Jack had the flu last week. I think there is a bug going around. Anne is due in another month. If it's a boy, we are going to name him after me," I told David while I was ringing up a customer's bill.

"That is great. All we need is two Robert Lapcheks in the world," Dave said, and we both laughed out loud.

I told David, "Our apartment is too small for a family of five."

"I know. A lot people are going over to Staten Island since they built the Verazzano Narrows Bridge. There is a good real estate agent over in Staten Island that I know. I could ask him to look out for a nice house if you want me to."

"That sounds great. I am looking for at least a three bedroom, maybe a few years old. What will it cost me?" I asked nervously.

"You are looking in twenty-five thousand area," David said.

"Good. I will talk to you next week. Ease up on the turkey breasts. I can't afford you anymore," I laughed.

After work, I went straight to see how my dad was doing. My mom looked agitated. "What is wrong?" I asked her.

"Dad is not doing very well," she said.

I didn't want to give her more bad news, but I gently told her, "Anne and I need a bigger place. We are thinking of moving. I hear Staten Island is a nice place to raise a family. I don't want to leave Dad in his condition . . ."

"Dad will be fine. I am still capable of taking care of him. Your family comes first," Mom smiled.

I went to Dad and turned him on his side to give him a rub down. He gave me a great big smile. I told Mom I'd stop back tomorrow.

When I arrived home -- one flight up from my parents -- Jack greeted me with open arms. I picked him up and gave him a hug and kiss.

"How was your day?" Anne asked while preparing dinner.

I told Anne about my conversation with Dave.

"That sounds great, but what about your dad? We are going to be further away," Anne, said.

"I just told my mom about it and she was supportive. Anyway, I could check on them when I am working," I told Anne while I took my shoes off my aching feet.

"By the way, Maz called today. He wants you to call him."

I washed up, had dinner, and then gave Maz a call.

"What's up, kid?" Maz said on the phone.

I told him, "Meet me down at the Eighth Street Inn tonight about ten o'clock for a few beers."

22

Johnny was tending bar. "What will it be, Bobby?"

"Give me a Bud on tap."

As soon as I downed my beer, Tom and Maz walked in.

"Hello, Bobby. How's the family? I heard you're having your third child soon. Good luck," Tom said.

"They are a handful. You'll both be there soon," I laughed.

Maz married Janet a year ago. Tom and Lori dated heavily after the wedding. They married soon after.

"Hey, Johnny, give these two fine officers a couple of cold ones," I told Johnny who was waiting on other customers. Johnny was generous with the beers. He only charged us one beer for every third beer we ordered. The owner hadn't caught on yet.

"I'm going up to Greenville this week. You guys want to come up?" Johnny asked while backing us up with another beer.

"Definitely, I haven't seen Joey in a long time. What day are we going up?" I asked.

"Probably Wednesday."

"You in, Maz?" I asked.

"I'm in," Maz agreed.

"How's the 30th Precinct treating you?" I asked.

"We have been there for a while now and seen a lot of shit," Maz said.

"What is different about the 30th Precinct?" I was anxious to hear.

"Well the 30th precinct area covers the south of West 155th Street to north of West 133rd Street, west of Edgecombe Avenue to the Hudson River. It is a very small precinct. The precinct covers about two square miles. Most of the action takes place on Broadway. It's a lot different than the Broadway in midtown. Every block on Broadway there are drug dealers selling their goods. There is a new drug hitting the streets called crack-cocaine. It looks like a small white rock that the dealers put in a small vial. There are about five to six people hanging out together all dressed in the same type of clothing. They make it harder for you to tell who is carrying the drugs. If someone were selling drugs on another dealer's turf, they wouldn't think of stabbing or even shooting their rival. The drugs come in from third world countries. Columbia and the Dominican Republic are the most productive countries. The majority of the drug dealers are Dominican. The other night a drug dealer was stabbed right in the back on Broadway in front of twenty to thirty people. The victim went DOA on the way to Columbia Presbyterian Hospital. When we tried to question about ten witnesses they all had the same answers that they didn't see anything happen. I guess they were afraid of having a knife in their back if they squealed on the perp. If there are no witnesses the detectives have to rely on physical evidence and cameras that are located nearby the crime. When there is a stabbing or shooting and the victim is likely to die, and then our Crime Scene Unit is notified to respond to take pictures and preserve the evidence. I talked to one of the detectives last night and the case on this drug dealer is still pending.

The 30th precinct also has the incidents that we call home invasions. Like Captain McGuire mentioned to us before we went up to the 30th precinct. Tom and I were patrolling in our assigned RMP when a call of shots fired at 610 West 144th Street came over the radio. You kind of get a premonition that it is a home invasion because of the way the job comes over the radio. Another sector was on the scene. The officer assigned to that sector transmitted over the radio that a male was tied up lying on the floor with a gunshot wound to his head. A person that lived in the next apartment observed two male Hispanics, one six foot tall wearing a blue jacket with the name Sisco on the back and the other perp was a male Hispanic about five foot eight wearing a plain black jacket and blue jeans. The witness then looked out the window and saw the perps get into a Honda Accord. However, there was no direction of flight on the Accord. We didn't know whether or not to believe the witness's story. Like I said before these people do not want to get involved. Tom and I parked our RMP on Riverside Drive and West 151st Street. Riverside Drive is the last street before anyone could drive onto the West Side Highway. There the perps could go north on the highway towards upstate or south towards lower Manhattan. I was betting that the perps would travel north to try and get out of the city. The George Washington Bridge was only seven blocks away. They could take the bridge and proceed into New Jersey. We asked our dispatcher to contact the Port Authority police to keep them aware of the situation. The George Washington Bridge was another area that the Port Authority Police patrolled along with the bus depot. We stayed on Riverside Drive and west 151st Street for about ten minutes. We didn't see any Honda Accord go past us. We decided to drive around the immediate area. We observe two men fitting the descriptions getting out of a parked Honda Accord on Riverside Drive and West 147th Street. Tom stops the RMP and we both jump out of the car. The two perps start running down Riverside Drive into Riverside Park. Riverside Park is adjacent to Riverside Drive. The park is huge. The park starts at West 135th Street and continues to West 185th Street near the George Washington Bridge. I transmitted over the radio that my partner and I were in pursuit of the two perps wanted in the home invasion. We are still in the park. The two perps are approaching a fence that separates the Metro North Railroad train tracks from the park. On the other side of the railroad tracks there is another fence that separates the tracks with the West Side Highway. Both perps start climbing the fence. Tom and I are just twenty-five feet behind them. The fence itself is twenty feet high. The perps are now over the fence. Tom makes it over. I am at the top of the fence when I feel a tug on my pants. My left pants leg is caught on the top portion of the fence. Not wasting any time, I rip my pants and jump to the ground. Blood is coming from a cut to my leg. We are now on the railroad tracks heading north. Tom and I are about thirty feet behind the perps. I ask the dispatcher on the radio to notify Metro North to discontinue service on the train line. One of the perps then makes a quick right hand turn and starts to climb this fifty foot cliff of embedded rocks that leads back to River Side Drive. I tell Tom that I am going to follow him and for Tom to follow the other perp. My perp is about forty feet up and I am about twenty feet behind him on the cliff when I see the perp start to loose his grip. He falls backwards so fast in a second he hits the ground below. I climb down from the cliff and walk over to him. He is bleeding from his head and not moving. There is a huge boulder near his head. I call for ambulance forthwith. I said to myself this is great now I am going to have to answer to our Internal Affairs Bureau and be interviewed all night long. I hear over the radio that Tom has caught the other perp at West 161st Street and River Side Drive. Emergency Medical Service now arrives and they pronounce the perp dead. I go with the ambulance to Columbian Presbyterian Hospital to have my leg checked out. The doctor diagnosed the injury as a small laceration. I went back to the 30th precinct to get grilled by the rats from the Internal Affairs Bureau. The interview is called a GO-15 hearing. If the Internal Affairs Bureau finds there is some criminal action, the Bureau then refers the case to the District Attorney. Since they found no criminal wrongdoing the Bureau then handles the case them-selves. The case is assigned two investigators. The investigators then question you on what happened during the incident at the GO-15 hearing. I told the Investigators what happened, that the perp fell after he lost his grip while climbing up the wall. Sometimes the Investigators believe your story and sometimes they don't. The Bureau investigates the case for about a couple of months. Then the he closes the case as being unsubstantiated or substantiated. If the investigator finds the case substantiated, you can go anywhere from losing your job or having some of your vacation days taken away. If the case comes back unsubstantiated, it means the incident did happen but there was not enough of sufficient evidence to jam you up. This part of the job sucks because you are doing your job and the department still takes you through hell. In all fairness it could have been me who fell from the cliff."

Maz said to Tom, "Tell Bobby what happened a few weeks ago."

"What happened a few weeks ago?" Tom asked.

"You know, the car stop we had," Maz said, looking like *who couldn't remember an incident like that.*

"Oh Yeah. Maz and I were conducting cars stops for red light summons. We stopped this beat up old Cadillac with an expired New York State registration. There were two Hispanics in the car. They were both acting nervously when I walked over to the driver and asked him for his license, Insurance card and registration. He gave me his license but had no registration or Insurance card. Maz who is standing on the passenger's side looks in the back seat and sees two empty beer cans. This now gives us probable cause to search the auto and the two Hispanics. Maz then asks them to get out of the car. I search the driver while Maz searches the passenger. We don't find any contraband on them. I then ask the driver to open the trunk of the car. These two were still acting nervous, which raised our suspicion. In fact the driver hands were shaking when he opened the trunk. There wasn't any contraband in plain sight. However, when Maz moved the box from the trunk there was an extremely large amount of cocaine and a couple of firearms underneath the box. Then the driver tells us to look in another box that was in the trunk. I open the box and see that there are stacks of one hundred dollar bills. I ask the driver how much money is there. He says about thirty thousand dollars. Then he tells us that we could have all of the money if we let him and his amigo go. Maz and I look at each other. We tell them to put their hands on the car while Maz and I walk about ten feet to talk. Oh boy did we talk. We talked for about fifteen minutes. We really thought about taking the money but decided to listen to the advice our old Captain McGuire said. We also heard rumors that the Internal Affairs Bureau was doing some sting operation in the 30th precinct. We placed the two Hispanics under arrest and brought them back to the 30th precinct.

When we arrived at the 30th precinct the desk Sergeant said to us in a sarcastic way, boys you two are the first officers tonight that brought in money with the guns and drugs. Some of these guys just bring in guns and drugs. We all started to laugh when Captain Lopez walked behind the desk. The Captain told us, good collar officers. I want to see us in my office later.

When I told the Sergeant in private that the two perps tried to bribe us, he said that we should call the Internal Affairs Bureau to get the bribe on tape. A bribery collar looks good on your record. So Maz called the Internal Affairs Bureau. When the IAB arrived, one of the Investigators planted a wire underneath my shirt. I brought the driver into an empty room and told him that I changed my mind and will take the money now. This guy is so stupid that he offers me the money again. The boys from IAB now have the conversation on tape. And we look like heroes with a bribery arrest.

After I started to process the arrests. Maz and I walked into the Captain's office. Sit down boys, he told us. You two are doing a great job here in the 30th Precinct. Both of you are making many good quality arrests. There is a new unit the job is starting up. It is called the Cold Case Squad. The unit investigates crimes that happened years ago and investigators could not find sufficient evidence to close the case. It sounds like a good detail if you two are interested.

Maz and I practically jumped down the Captain's throat when he recommended the position to us. He said that the unit is starting in a few months and will put in a couple of good words for us.

We went out to Smith's bar that night to celebrate with a few other officers from the precinct. Maz told everyone that the drinks are on him for the rest of the night. I asked Maz, What gives? Maz said you know the bribery arrests we had tonight. I opened my eyes wide and my jaw practically dropped to the floor as he shows me a bill. Maz told me, relax I only borrowed a Ben Franklin. I laughed so loud. I think I was just relieved hopefully that Maz was telling the truth."

After a few more beers we all said goodnight, and I told Johnny that Maz and I would meet him Wednesday to go up to Greenville.

23

I opened the store late on Sunday. There were only a few customers. Everyone must have been at church. I was thinking of having the store closed on Sundays for good. I wasn't doing much business on Sundays.

I took little Jack to five o'clock mass at Our Lady of Help Church. Anne was feeling tired and there was no sense bringing Barbara since she cried at church all the time. There were more Spanish people attending mass. The church was half full with white and Spanish people. More and more Spanish people had been moving into the north side.

Jack and I stopped at Franks to grab a bite to eat. While we were having our dinner there was a Spanish man two tables away. The man was just staring at me menacingly for quite a while. I couldn't tell if it was Juan or just someone who looked like him. It had been years since the murder. The man had some scars on his face. I felt a little nervous with Jack there. The man finished his dinner, paid the bill, and left.

Jack and I finished our piazza and started to walk

home. I looked behind me on every block to see if the man was following me. When I arrived home I didn't tell Anne. I didn't want to get her nervous. Maybe it wasn't anything.

24

Maz and Johnny met me at the store about eleven o'clock on Wednesday. I told Charlie to take the register while Michael worked the deli.

I drove to Greenville. On the way there I told Maz about the incident at Frank's the other day.

"Did the guy say anything to you?" Maz asked.

"No, maybe it wasn't anything . . ."

"We will all go to Frank's next week to see what this guy wants," Johnny said, grinding his teeth.

We walked into Greenville. I took the lead; Johnny and Maz followed. It was tight security as usual.

We were walking in the hallway when this short, stocky man bumped into me. "Hey, I know you. You are Bobby Lapchek. You own the grocery store on North Seventh Street and Bedford Avenue."

"Yes I do," I said, not knowing the man.

"I am Tony Russo from North Tenth Street."

"Oh yeah, I have seen you around the neighborhood a few times."

"Your friend Joey is not doing so well," Tony said.

"What do you mean?'

"Well, let him tell you himself. Bobby, I'll stop by your store and check on you," Tony said.

"Don't do us any favors," Johnny said with a smirk.

I jumped in. "Sure, Tony. I'll see you around."

I asked Johnny, "What does he mean, I'll be checking on you? All I need is this grease ball showing up at my store wanting a cut from my profits."

Johnny put his hand on my shoulder, "Don't worry, Bobby, I'll take care of it."

We walked to the visitors' room. Joey was already there. "Glad to see you fellas," Joey said with a smile. "Tony Russo was just here. Did you see him?"

"Yeah, we just bumped into him on our way here. What is going on? He said that you have bad news for us?" I asked Joey.

"I tuned this guy up pretty good the other day. He keeps giving me a hard time. The asshole warden wants to hit me up with an assault charge. He said that could add on a couple more years to my sentence. I told you that prick hated my guts," Joey said, sitting back in his chair.

"How many more years is that?" I asked.

"That's about eight more years I have to serve," Joey answered.

"Come on, Joey, what's going on?" Johnny pleaded.

"I guess this warden has it in for me," Joey said, looking away from us. "Enough about me. How is the family, Bobby? I heard you're on your third child."

"I'm stopping at three. Two is a handful. Anne and I are thinking of moving to the suburbs, maybe Staten Island. We need more room," I told Joey.

"How is the police department treating you, Maz? Johnny tells me that you are in Harlem," Joey said with a smile.

"Harlem is a shit hole. There are loads of drugs and plenty of shootings," Maz said half-heartily.

"Be careful out there," Joey said sincerely.

The time went quick. The corrections officer came over and told us it was time to leave. We all shook Joey's hand and hugged him, leaving with a guilty feeling again.

25

Dave carried the cold cuts in the store. "Bobby, I talked to my buddy Sam the real estate agent. He wants you and Anne to come to Staten Island tonight. He has a great house for you guys to look at."

"I'll tell Anne to get a babysitter for the kids." My mother-in-law could watch them. That was also our plan: we would have Anne's mother live with us in Staten Island now that she was now living alone. She could watch the kids while Anne and I worked.

Anne and I met Sam at the real estate office. "Dave told me that you were coming. I have a wonderful house for you two to look at. It is in the middle of Staten Island but close to the Verrazano Bridge."

The Verrazano Bridge was just completed. Before, everyone had to take the Staten Island ferry to get on and off of the island.

When we arrived at the house Anne instantly fell in love with it. It was an all-brick ranch with four bedrooms and a finished basement.

"This is a beautiful house, and it is reasonably priced,"

Sam said with a wide smile on his face, knowing he was going to get a commission.

We went back to his office to make an offer on the house. "I will get back to you during the week. You two better move fast with the bridge being completed more and more people are moving here," Sam said as we shook hands.

When I arrived back home, I got a call from Maz. "Bobby, I have great news to tell you. I don't want to tell you over the phone. I'm coming to the store tomorrow." He then hung up the phone.

26

It was noon when Maz came into the store. "Bobby, lets go over to the Inn and have lunch," he said.

I got Charlie to watch the register, and we made our way over to the Inn. We both ordered the cheeseburger deluxe and a beer.

"I made this collar yesterday for fifty ounces of cocaine," Maz said.

"Is that a lot?" I asked.

"It sure is. Anyway, I processed my arrest at the precinct then went downtown to draw it up. The arrest room was crowded as usual. When my name was called by the Assistant District Attorney to draw up the case, he told me to come with him to his office. He must have been new because he didn't realize the weight of the cocaine and couldn't decide on the charge. He wanted to talk to his supervisor. The supervisor's office was across the street. So we walked across the street to his supervisor's office. The building was quite old, probably over one hundred years. It contained many offices and some courtrooms. We took the elevator to the twentieth floor where all the supervisors had their offices. When we walked into his supervisor's office my heart was pounding like a drum. The supervisor looked exactly like Adam Morley. Then I looked at the nameplate on the desk. The nameplate read Adam Morley, Supervisor, Special Narcotics.

"Adam didn't recognize me at first, then he looked at me again. He screamed out loud, 'Holy Shit, Billy!' We embraced each other.

I said to Adam I didn't know you worked in District Attorney's Office? He said he was working in the District Attorney's Office for about three years. He told me I didn't know I was a police officer? I told him I was a cop for ten years. We talked about the job for a while and then he asked how you and Joey are doing. I informed him that Joey was still up at Greenville and wasn't doing very well. The warden up there hates him and is trying to have Joey serve time. I went on to tell him that you have two kids and are expecting your third real soon. I also mentioned that you bought the building across the street from the old restaurant and opened a grocery store on the ground floor. He wants to get together with us soon. He said probably in a couple of weeks. Adam also wants to go up to Greenville to visit Joey."

"That sounds great, Maz." I was glad to hear that Adam was back and couldn't wait to see him.

27

Two weeks later I went to Maz's house. Maz lived in Astoria, Queens. Astoria was mostly a residential neighborhood. Many cops lived in Queens. Maz lived in a modest townhouse on a nice quiet block. Maz told me that he invited Adam over. I couldn't wait to see him. Janet was at work in Manhattan. They were expecting their first child.

Maz and I had a cup of coffee when the doorbell rang. It was Adam. Adam and I first looked at each other for a few seconds, and then threw our arms around each other. "Adam, you look the same as you did fifteen years ago. I am sure glad to see you again. How was school down south?" I asked, still trying to calm down from the excitement of seeing him.

"I went to Georgetown University for six years. I received my law degree there. Law school was hard. I started to work at a law firm in Washington. The pay was decent there but I was getting a little homesick, so I decided to come back to New York and landed in the Manhattan District Attorney's office. I have an apartment in lower Manhattan near the courthouses. It's convenient to get to work. I've been supervisor of the Special Narcotics Bureau for a year now. The District Attorney himself told me that his assistant is leaving soon and that I could take his spot. That is second in charge. Enough of about me, how the hell are you doing, Bobby? Maz tells me that you bought the apartment building across the street from your dad's old restaurant and opened up a grocery store. And you married Anne and have two kids with another on the way," Adam said while pouring himself a cup of coffee.

I told him, "The grocery business is doing well. The kids are great. Jack is three years old and Barbara is almost a year old. Anne is doing well with our third child due in a few weeks. We are growing out of our apartment so we are thinking of buying ourselves a house. We made an offer on a house in Staten Island. I hope it comes through."

"How is your dad doing?" Adam asked.

"Not so good, he can hardly walk and has to be fed almost all the time," I told Adam.

Maz jumped in. "You guys ready? It is about a three hour ride to Greenville."

As we approached Greenville, Adam asked, "Why is Joey having such a hard time in here?"

Maz said, "I think he keeps on getting into fights; and you know Joey, he doesn't back down from any shit. He said the warden hates him. He tries to keep on adding more years to his sentence by bringing him up on assault charges."

"His parents never go up to visit him. Tony Russo from the neighborhood visits him often. They became good friends," I told Adam. I could see some guilt on Adam's face.

"That no-good hoodlum. We have to somehow talk some sense into Joey."

We arrived at Greenville. I asked the guard if we could visit Joey Bettino. We waited a while before a guard brought Joey from his cell. I could see Joey's knees buckling when he saw Adam. "Holy shit, what brings an important man like you to this shit hole?" Joey said, trying to act like a tough guy.

"What's up, buddy?" Adam said.

"Johnny told me the other day that you are a big-shot lawyer, Adam. Can you get me out of here?" Joey laughed.

"No, Joey, I just work in the Manhattan District Attorney's office. How are they treating you in here? I understand you are having a tough time of it. Do you want me to talk to the warden and see if there is anything I can do?"

"No way, that asshole wouldn't give me the time of day . . . and anyway I can take care of myself in here."

Adam asked Joey, "What the hell are you doing with that guy Tony Russo?"

"He comes up to visit me all the time. Tony also looks out for me in here. If it wasn't for him I'd probably be dead by now."

We all talked to Joey for a while, then Adam said, "Maz and I are thinking of a way to get you out of here."

"Get me out of here?" Joey said, startled.

As soon as Adam started to explain, the guard came in. "Time's up."

Adam pulled out his identification. "I am an attorney with the Manhattan District Attorney's office. I need more time to talk to my friend --"

"I don't care who you are. The three of you have to leave now."

"You see what I mean, they don't give a rat's ass about anything in here," Joey said as the guard escorted him to his cell.

Adam told Joey, "We will see you soon."

As we were driving back to Maz's house, I asked, "What's this plan you have?"

"I just received word that Tom and I are going into the new unit called the Cold Case Squad." Maz tells me.

I said, "Oh yeah."

The unit digs up old cases. I might get a chance to dig up Joey's old case and you never know what could happen. Adam, you can help me on Joey's case since you are working in the District Attorney's Office."

Adam says, "That sounds like a good plan but I may have a better plan if that doesn't work. I plan to run for Governor, a position that can grant a pardon."

I told Maz, "Be careful with your plan, Maz, you don't want to open a can of worms. Remember who really committed the murder. I think I like Adam's plan better."

28

The commute from Staten Island to the grocery store was horrible. I had to leave my house on the island around 5:30 in the morning just to beat some of the traffic. It still took me over an hour to get into Greenpoint. I usually hit some traffic on the Brooklyn-Queens Expressway around the Brooklyn Bridge. And forget about going home. I closed the store at 6:00 in the afternoon and sometimes didn't pull into my driveway until 7:30 p.m.

We had been living in our house for five years. It is a four-bedroom house with a finished basement and a modest backyard. Anne's mother was living with us. Veronica did most of the housework, cleaning, cooking, and babysitting for all three kids. This gave Anne a chance to work so we could have a little extra money. Anne commuted to the city. She did secretarial work at an accounting firm.

Every day at work I took a break for an hour and went upstairs to see how my parents were doing. My dad was still hanging in there, but he could hardly move without help. I asked my mom, "Why don't you and Dad come over and live with Anne and I? The basement is finished and we have plenty of room."

"Robert, you have your hands full with the three children. Anyway, I see you practically every day, and you are downstairs working in the store if Dad or I need you. Have you seen Ashley and Courtney lately?"

Ashley and Courtney had both married and moved to Staten Island a couple of years after Anne and I. "No, I haven't. I've been busy with the store and the kids," I told my mother.

While I was leaving to go back to the store, I saw a man across the street staring at the building. It looked like the guy I saw five years ago at Frank's Pizzeria, but it was hard for me to tell with the glare from the sun in my eyes. I started to walk across the street, but the man turned around and started to walk away from me at a fast pace southbound on Bedford Avenue. I started to walk fast too. There were many pedestrians on the streets. A middle-aged man yelled to me, "Where the fuck are you going?" when I practically knocked him down. I was about a block behind the man on Bedford Avenue between North Sixth Street and North Fifth Street when I saw him jump into the passenger seat of a dark blue Chevy Oldsmobile. I only saw the back of two heads as the Chevy sped south down Bedford Avenue. I couldn't make out the license plate number. I wondered again if it was Juan.

I walked back to the store. Charlie was working the register. "Bobby, it looks like you seen a ghost. Are you all right?"

I took a seat near the register. "Yeah, it must be the hot sun."

As I arrived home from work and opened the door, little Robert greeted me with a big hug and kiss. Veronica was preparing dinner. We all sat down at the table. Anne asked me, "How was work today?"

I told her, "Good," not wanting to get her worried about the man I saw. "But there are less and less customers coming to the store as the days go by. I think we are losing some customers to the bigger supermarkets. A&B just opened a huge store on Grand Street. I hear some of our customers say that it is worth traveling a few more blocks to save a couple of dollars."

As we finished dinner the phone rang. It was Al Falco. "What's up, buddy? Are you still interested in designer clothes?"

Al operated a warehouse down in the East Village in lower Manhattan. He dealt with retailers and bought these designer clothes and other apparel real cheap. I thought most of the merchandise fell off a truck. He wanted me to sell them in the store to supplement my income. "Al, with the store not doing so well, I think I will take you up on your offer."

"Good, Bobby. Then I will see you on Sunday at the warehouse."

29

Manhattan was desolate on a Sunday morning. The only people on the street were the homeless waking up to have their hangovers greet them from a drunken Saturday night. Most of the businesses were closed or opened late on Sunday. I decided to close my store that day. I'd been opening two Sundays out of the month. Maybe Al's merchandise would help business.

Al's warehouse was on Vesey Street, a block from the Hudson River in SoHo. It was a six-floor building that stored all kinds of goods, from clothing to house ware to dry foods.

I knocked on the steel gate. The rattling sound must have been heard for a couple of blocks. As the gate opened, there was Al standing alone on the shipping dock. "Come in, Bobby. We're the only two people in the building."

We took the freight elevator to the third floor. The old elevator was rocking back and forth. We reached the third floor, and Al took about ten dresses off a rack. "These are designer dresses. They are not knock-offs. I also have some designer pocketbooks. You could make a good buck selling them."

"Thanks. I'll take a dozen dresses and pocketbooks to start with. I want to see if they sell first before I buy more," I said as I paid him. We headed back downstairs.

"Let me know if you want more," Al said as he looked around while closing the gate. I got in my car and drove back home.

Monday morning I started to display the clothing and pocketbooks. My customers started to come back during the week. In fact, they kept asking when I was going to get more new merchandise. I meet Al every other Sunday at his warehouse to buy more goods. During the next couple of months I could see the grocery business pick up.

Tony Russo strolled in one Tuesday afternoon. "Bobby, what's this I hear about you making a killing on selling dresses and other merchandise?"

"I purchased the goods from a retail store down on Delancey Street in lower Manhattan," I lied. I didn't want Tony to know where I really purchased the merchandise. "I don't make much of a profit off of the goods, but my regular customers are coming back to buy groceries."

Tony was deep in thought. "Come on, Bobby, you wouldn't have that many customers buying that many groceries in such a short period of time. You can't fool me."

"No, that is the truth, Tony."

I could see Tony getting a little red in the face and gritting his teeth. "So, you are not going to tell me where you buy these goods? Alright then, you'll see what'll happen," Tony said while walking out the door.

I said to myself, *Great, now I have Tony Russo pissed at*

me and I don't even know who the man that keeps staring at my store is.

As soon as Tony walked out of the store Maz came walking in, "What did that schmuck Russo want? If he is bothering you, Bobby, let me know, I'll take care of it."

"He asked me if I wanted go to the policeman's ball."

"Funny, Bobby." We both laughed.

"How is the job going? Are you still in the Cold Case Squad?" I asked.

"I sure am. I think I found my niche. There is a case I am working on. That's why I dropped in. I have to interview a witness in the neighborhood. A serial killer back in the late seventies may have killed three young children in the span of two years. I am also trying to get Joey's case open. But my lieutenant is asking me many questions on why I want to open that case. Joey did plead guilty. The evidence is in an old warehouse in Queens called Pierson Place. That is where the department stores all old property and evidence. The only people assigned there are civilians and cops who get jammed up on the job. So I am thinking of a way to screw up."

"That shouldn't be hard," I laughed. "Be careful, Maz. Adam is running for governor in November. I am sure he will take care of Joey."

"Yeah, I know, but we don't know if he'll make it. His opposition is pretty tough," Maz said. "I have to run now. Lets get together on Saturday. We'll go out for a few drinks and steaks at Peter Logan's. Just the men. I'll call Adam. Let's make it early, say around four o'clock. Right after you close the store."

"That sounds great to me."

30

I closed the store at three-thirty on Saturday. I told Charlie that I would see him on Monday, and then I drove to Peter Logan's. I walked in, looked around, and did not see Maz or Adam, so I decided to have a drink at the bar. Peter Logan's hadn't changed. The furniture still looked like it was from the sixties, and they still put sawdust on the floor. I took a quick glance at the menu and saw that the prices did change. They practically doubled. I finished my glass of Johnny Walker Red when Maz and Adam walked in together.

"Congratulations, Governor," I told Adam as I shook his hand.

"No, no, Bobby not just yet. Although it has a nice sound to it."

We sat at a quiet table in the back of the restaurant. The waiter recognized Adam and knew that he wanted to be out of the public eye. The waiter wished Adam good luck in the election. Although our table was well hidden people still came up to Adam and wished him good luck.

"Maz, tell Adam your plan about the evidence on Joey's case," I said.

"Like I told Bobby the other day, I was thinking of being transferred to the property clerk's office in Queens where all the old evidence is located. The job only lets cops on modified assignment work there. That means I would have to get my guns taken away --"

Adam jumped in. "You don't have to do that, Maz. The commissioner is a friend of mine. I can talk to him and have you transferred there."

"That would look suspicious. Anyway, I had an argument with my lieutenant the other day. He didn't like the way I was handling the Grove case. Adam, you remember the case with the three dead children that were murdered back in 1972 and 1973."

The waiter brought us three huge, delicious looking steaks. "I vaguely remember. Why don't you tell me more on the case?"

"Jason Grove was walking to school one day in the Throgs-Neck section of the Bronx. He only lived three blocks away from his school. He never showed up for school. Don't ask me why, but the principal did not call the police until ten o'clock. Valuable amount of time went by. Jason's mother worked during the day at a florist, but the school had an old number for the florist store. His father was out of the picture a long time ago. The police do a grid search of the area and came up with nothing. Two people hiking in the woods found his body one month later in Pelham Bay Park. Well, part of his body anyway. The boy was mutilated. Jason was only twelve years old. The mother was questioned along with a couple of neighbors, but nobody saw a thing. His mother said she was running late for work and didn't have time to walk Jason to school. The detectives tried to get in touch with his father but they couldn't locate him. We have a tip on where he might be living now. That is what my lieutenant and I are fighting about. He thinks it is a waste of time while I think it is a reliable tip. I just might have to punch him in the head."

Maz continued as he was chewing on his delicious steak. "Another child was found dead, washed up on a jetty on City Island about five months later. The body was so badly decomposed the detectives never identified it. The coroner said that it was a boy, probably around eleven years old. The third body was found in a landfill under the Throgs-Neck Bridge. Some construction workers who were about to start building apartment complexes found the body.

"This time it was an eight-year old female. The medical examiner said she was sexually assaulted before she was strangled. In fact, he thinks all the children were sexually assaulted before they were murdered."

I asked Maz, "What happened to her case -- did the detectives question anyone?"

"They questioned the toll collectors that worked on the bridge. One toll collector saw a white male running from the landfill two days before the girl's body was found. The toll collector never came forward because he didn't think it was important. The detectives never found any suspects. I was looking over the residents that live on City Island, and there appears to be a couple of pedophiles that live on the island. I am going to question them. Adam, you need to hang this guy if I find him!"

"Just find this prick and I will take care of the rest," Adam stated while he was finishing his steak.

I asked Adam, "Is there anything new in the D. A.'s office?"

Adam replied, "Well, Bobby, now that you ask, I am working with the Feds and going to try to indict the Masimino Family on racketeering and conspiracy charges. They control most of the shipping industry at the docks. A couple of owners from the shipping company were found floating in the Hudson Bay. Rumor has it that they didn't like the way things were being handled and were going to the police to rat out on the family. In fact, one of the owners was wearing a wire."

"Tony Russo is a member of that family."

Yes, I know, Bobby. That's the idea. Maybe we could get some of the family to turn on each other," Adam said with a smile. "Let me put the dinner on my expense account," he said as the waiter handed him the check. "Bobby, when you get the chance come and visit me down town at the office. We'll have lunch together."

"I think I will take you up on the offer."

We all shook hands and said goodnight.

31

Sweat was pouring from my face as I finished cutting my grass. It usually took me about two hours to mow and trim the lawn. The temperature was in the nineties at six o'clock in the afternoon. It was a Saturday, a time to unwind from another week of work. I closed the store a little early that day. Anne took the kids along with her mother to her friend Sarah's house on the other side of the island.

I took a shower and was about to sit down and watch the baseball game with a beer when the doorbell rang. It was Sean Flynn, a neighbor that lived down the block. I think Sean was in the Irish Mafia the way he talked. Sean was a short and slim man. He always wanted to get in the action, game for anything.

"Sean, grab a beer and come down to the basement. I am about to watch the stinking New York Mets. They are still in last place."

"Bob, are you going into the city tomorrow to Al's warehouse? I need to buy some clothes from him. I have to pay the bills too," Sean asked as the Mets fell behind three to zero.

I told Sean," No, I am kind of tired. You can go yourself. I'm sure Al won't mind."

"Can I bring my friend Lenny?".

"Is Lenny the consigliore?" I teased

"No, Bob, he is a good friend of mine," Sean said, getting a little annoyed with me.

To change his mood, I told Sean, "I have another friend to introduce to you. His name is Sol. He is Jewish and sells fine jewelry. Sol's business is located in Williamsburg. He is coming to the store on Wednesday this week. I'll introduce him to you, if you want to come by."

"Sure, you know you can count me in, Bobby."

Sean and I started on the Johnny Walker after we finished the six-pack of beer. I talked about the good buys I was making from Al's merchandise. Then Anne and the kids came home around eleven o'clock.

"Bobby, I will see you on Wednesday," Sean said to me as he polished off his drink and stumbled out the front door.

"How much did you two drink?" asked Anne, pissed off.

"Did you kids have a good time?" I asked the kids, slurring my words.

"Give Daddy a big kiss good-night."

I went to bed knowing that the Mets lost again by a score of ten to one.

The next morning I woke up to the sound of the telephone. It was ten o'clock. Everybody slept late on Sunday morning. My head was pounding to the beat of a drum. I answered the phone.

"What's up, kid?" Maz said.

"Did you have to call so early on a Sunday morning?"

"I have good news for you, Bobby. I got transferred to the property clerk's office last week."

"How did you do it? I hope you didn't get in real serious trouble."

"You know that lieutenant I was telling you about --" Maz started.

"You need not tell me anything further."

"Anyway, it's hard to find any particular kind of evidence. Five of the six floors in the building contain files of evidence and the building is a square block long. The office opens at six o'clock in the morning and closes at six o'clock in the evening. There are always civilians or other cops working. My sergeant is always lurking around too."

I told Maz, "Be careful. You are already on modified duty and you may lose your job if you get caught."

"You know the difference between you and me, Bobby?"

"No, what is the difference between you and I, Maz?" I asked him, already knowing the answer.

"The difference between us is that you worry too much, Bobby."

I could hear Maz laughing hard on the other end of the phone. "I have to make breakfast for the kids."

Maz said, "I will call you in a couple of weeks and tell you how I made out."

I hung up the phone hoping thickheaded Maz would not get in any more trouble.

32

Wednesday morning was quiet. My food delivery came every Wednesday morning. I seemed to be purchasing less and less groceries than before. The customers were buying groceries months ago, but now they were buying mostly the clothing.

Sean entered the store. "Hey, Bob, I made Al a rich man on Sunday. I practically bought all of his merchandise."

"Good, but I hope you saved some for me. It is getting harder to make a living on just the grocery business."

I could see the anxiety on Sean's face when he asked me, "Where is your friend Sol?"

"Relax Sean, he should be here in a couple of minutes. Go in the back and tell Charlie to make you a sandwich." Sean took me up on the offer.

A few minutes later Sol walked in the store. "Bobby how was your weekend?"

"It was pretty good, and yours?"

Sol was a tall gentleman, about six-four, with a heavy build and a long beard. Of course, he was wearing his yarmulke. Sol was in his mid-forties. "I went to my summer house in the Catskills. It's beautiful up there. The summer nights are nice and cool. The kids and I did a little fishing and swimming in the lake. One weekend you should bring the wife and kids up. We'll have a blast."

"Maybe I will one weekend," I said as Sean walked up front chomping on a roast beef sandwich.

Sean shook Sol's hand. "Bob has been telling me that you have a jewelry business in Williamsburg."

"I am sorry, Sol, this is my friend Sean from Staten Island. Sean is in the retail business." I wasn't even sure what Sean did for a living.

"Nice to met you, Sean," Sol smiled. "Yes, I have a store in Williamsburg. Would you like to come and look at my merchandise?"

"Sure, I would love to. Can I come over now?" Sean asked.

"Follow me in your car. It is only a few minutes from here." Sol said. "Bobby, I will call you at the end of the week."

Sean winked at me. "Bob, I'll stop over the house on the weekend."

I thought, *Sean is up to no good.*

The weekend couldn't come fast enough. I didn't hear from Sol, and I hoped Sean behaved himself. I didn't want to lose a customer and a good friend.

Anne went shopping with her mother, Jack, and Barbara. Little Robert was watching television in his room.

The doorbell rang. I knew that it was Sean. We grabbed a few beers and went in the backyard.

"Where are Anne and the kids?"

"They went shopping for clothes," I told Sean.

"What's the matter, Al's stuff isn't good enough for her?"

I laughed. "Did you make any good buys from Sol on Wednesday?"

"Listen, Bobby, we are thinking of hitting him --"

"Hitting him? What do you mean *hitting him*?"

"Well . . . you know, Bobby, robbing him. His store is located in front of his house. I ask Sol if I could take a piss. He tells me that his bathroom is in back of his house on the first floor. He must live on the second floor and use the first floor for business. There is an office right next to the bathroom. So I am about to flush the toilet when I look through a crack in the door and see Sol put a stack of money and some jewelry in his safe. His jewelry is excellent quality. I cased the place out. The store has a burglar alarm but the back office doesn't; and I know the Jewish people go up to the Catskills every weekend during the summer. I talked to Lenny and he says he is in. What about you, Bobby?"

"Leave me out of this, Sean. I think you should think this over. Sol is a gentleman. I don't want to lose a good friend and customer --"

"How is he going to know it's us, Bobby? He will be away."

"This doesn't sound too good, Sean . . ." I said

"Well, it's a done deal. Lenny and I are thinking of doing it this weekend." Sean seemed disappointed with me as he jumped up from his chair.

I grabbed him and practically threw him out of the yard "Make sure you leave me out of this mess!"

The next day I was feeling guilty about introducing Sean to Sol. I had to let Sol know somehow that Sean was going to rob him, but it would look bad if I came straight out and told him that Sean was going to steal his money.

I had it!

I called Sol on the phone. "Sol, it is Bobby."

"How is it going, Bobby?"

"Sol, a man came into the store today and asked me if I wanted to buy some quality jewelry. I told him I that I don't deal in jewelry but I knew a man that was in the jewelry business. I told him I took a look at the merchandise and it looked like excellent quality. He said he could meet you this weekend. Are you interested?"

"Bobby, you know I go up to the Catskills on the weekends. Can I meet him during the week?"

"No, he travels during the week and deals his jewelry on the side on weekends, usually on Sundays," I told Sol. Sean was thinking of hitting his house on early Sunday morning. I was hoping Sol would be at home all weekend.

"Alright, Bobby, tell him I will meet him over the weekend; but not at my house, and it has to be on Sunday. The Sabbath is on Saturday. We'll meet in a parking lot," Sol said.

"Good, I will tell him to meet you at the high school parking lot on early Sunday. By the way, his name is Abraham." I knew the Jewish people trusted each other.

The rest of the week went slowly. It was finally Saturday and I was feeling guilty. To get my mind off of Sean and

Sol, I called Al and told him that I would meet him in the city tomorrow to buy some of his merchandise.

Sean and Sol were still on my mind, so I took a bottle of Johnnie Walker from my bar and sat down and watched the Mets game. They were getting clobbered again, seven to two and it was only the fifth inning.

The next thing I knew the sun was beating down on my face through the window. There was a blanket on top of me and the television was off. Anne must have put the blanket on top of me. My head was pounding. I looked at the bottle of Johnnie Walker and it was practically finished. I walked over to the cabinet and took three aspirin for my headache.

"It must have been a rough night. I think you need some of this," Anne said as she walked into the kitchen and started to make the coffee. "Are you going over to see Al this morning?"

"Oh, shit, what time is it?" I asked.

"Ten o'clock."

"I was supposed to meet Al at ten o'clock at the warehouse. I'll call him and tell him that I am running a little late."

I called Al, finished my breakfast, and took a quick shower. I pulled up to the warehouse and met Al at the docking bay.

"Lets go up to the third floor, Bobby. I have some new clothing that just came in." Al said while we got into the elevator. "Don't you have a friend named Sol that you do business with in Williamsburg?" Al asked as my face turned white.

Why is Al asking about Sol? "Yes . . ."

"I heard on the radio coming in this morning that

there was a burglary at his house last night and that he was killed trying to stop it."

My heart just fell to the ground. "Did they give any more information on the incident? Did the police catch the persons who did it?" I asked Al.

"No, the newscaster didn't say if it was one or more persons that did it. How well did you know this guy Sol?"

I was wondering if Al was getting suspicious when I asked him if the police caught the persons who did it. "We only did business a couple of times," I told Al, looking away.

"Well, I am sorry to hear that he passed away. Send my regards to his family." Al said, shaking my hand.

On the drive back to Staten Island a million things were going through my mind at a time. Why were Sean and Sol at the house on Saturday night? Saturday was the Sabbath. Sol said he wasn't going to be home on Saturday. How did Sol die? Did the police know that Sean did it? I couldn't wait any longer. The minute I got home I was going to call Sean.

I made it back from Manhattan in about thirty minutes, a trip that usually takes about an hour. Anne left a note saying that she went to her friend's house to take the kids swimming. I called Sean on the phone. "What the fuck happened?" I yelled at him.

"I am sorry, Bobby. I don't want to talk about it over the phone. Why don't you meet me in my backyard?"

I told Sean that I would be right over. I didn't want to be seen going into Sean's house in case the police were watching his house so I walked through the backyard.

When I arrived, Sean was already sitting down on a wicker chair with his head down. He looked up at me and said, "I am sorry, Bobby," one more time. "I didn't know that fat fuck was going to be home. Everything was going beautiful. Lenny and I cased the place before we went in. There were no cars in the driveway and we didn't see anyone in the house. Lenny picked a back window near the office. We made our way inside. We went straight to the safe where Sol kept his money. Lenny starts to pick the safe lock. You know Lenny is good at picking locks. We hear a noise coming from upstairs. Then I hear someone coming down the stairs. Believe me, those sounds were loud. Lenny and I are hiding in the back kitchen. We both look at each other when we see that fat prick Sol. Sol walks through the kitchen and into the office. I could see him look around all puzzled. I motion to Lenny: *lets get the fuck out of here*. As soon as we make a run to the door Sol sees us. He runs to the door first.

"Now, here is this three-hundred-pound gorilla between the door and Lenny and me. 'Where do you think you two are going?' Sol said. I didn't know what to say. He told us that he was calling the police. We tried pushing out of the way but he wouldn't budge. The next thing I know Lenny puts his arms around Sol's neck and I try to grab his legs from under him so he would fall. Sol throws Lenny about five feet to the ground. Now I am trying to bring this gorilla down by myself. He starts to fall backwards real fast. He ends up hitting his head on a marble table that was near the door. I see blood gushing out of his head and he is not breathing. We were thinking of trying to make it look like a suicide, but it was hard since that fat fuck landed on the back of his head. We didn't even get a chance to take the money. If only that fat prick wasn't home."

Now I am feeling even guiltier by making Sol stay home. "Do you think the police have an idea it was you and Lenny?"

Sean had his head down again. "No way, Bobby. Lenny and I made it very clean. We both wore gloves and wiped everything down. I watched the news before and they said that the police have very little evidence and no suspects."

I pointed my finger at Sean, "Lay low for a while. Try not to call me unless it is absolutely necessary -- and do not come to my store at all. And stay away from Al. I do not want to lose another friend. I know it is going to be hard for a while . . ."

Sean agreed by trying to shake my hand but I refused. "Bobby, you will not see me for a while."

33

A few months passed and I hadn't heard from Sean. I guess it was a good sign that the police never came to my door and asked any questions about Sol.

It was nine o'clock on a Tuesday morning when Maz walked in the store. I asked him if he'd heard anything about the murder of the jewelry man in Williamsburg a few months ago.

Maz looked startled. "No. I heard that there is not much evidence in the case and we have no suspects. Why, did you know this guy?"

"I did business with him a couple of times," I said. "Anyway, Maz, what brings you here early on a Tuesday morning?"

"Do you have a job for me? I am out on thirty-day suspension."

"What happened now?"

"I got in trouble at the property clerk's office. I was working there last Thursday. It was five o'clock in the evening when I thought everyone signed out and went home except one civilian and myself. Even my sergeant signed out. I knew it was a great opportunity to look up the evidence in Joey's case. It took me a while. I went floor to floor . . . there must have been three thousand boxes of evidence from other cases. I finally found the storage box that contained Joey's case. I looked in the box. I couldn't believe that the knife was still in the property bag after all these years. I started to open the bag when I look behind me and see my sergeant standing there. He asked me what the hell I was doing. I stood there speechless. He grabbed the bag from me and read the name on the tag. Then he tells me, 'You know, your old lieutenant told me to keep an eye on you. He told me that you were asking him questions about this case. You know, I could suspend you for tampering with evidence.' Well you know what, Bobby, he did. And don't tell me that you told me so."

"Are you going to lose you job?" I asked.

"I hope not. I have to talk to Adam. Maybe he could ask the police commissioner to spare me my job. Oh, by the way, you know what day it is?" Maz's said, his eyes wide. "It's election day. Let's give Adam a call and wish him luck."

"He is probably to busy with the election. I have to go to cast my vote. I'll stop on my way home."

"Yeah, I am going home now to vote," Maz said.

"Let me know how the suspension goes, Maz," I said as he walked out the door.

I stopped at the public school near my house to vote for Adam. While I waited to go into the booth a man tapped me on my shoulder. "Bobby Lapchek, right?"

I said to him, "I'm sorry?"

"It is Kevin, Adam Morley's cousin. We meet back when we were teenagers on the north side."

I looked at him more closely. "Yes, yes, now I remember."

"Boy, that was some night," Kevin said. "I guess you are here to vote for Adam? Me too. How is Joey doing? He served all his time?"

It was our turn to vote, but Kevin and I stepped back to let other people go ahead. "No, Kevin. Joey keeps getting into trouble. He has some more time to serve. The warden had him brought up on assault charges. We are hoping if Adam gets in he could help him."

"I keep in touch with Adam but he never mentions Joey," Kevin said. "How is your other friend doing?"

"You mean Maz. He's doing well. He is a detective with the New York City Police Department."

Kevin looked surprised.

I told Kevin, "Looks like it is my turn to vote."

"Bobby, let's get together one day. I live in Grant City. Let me give you my number." Kevin took a pen from the table and wrote his telephone number on piece of paper and handed it to me.

"I will give you a call next week. We could celebrate Adam's victory," I told Kevin as I headed into the booth to vote for Adam.

Anne had dinner on the table when I arrived home. I told her, "I stopped to vote for Adam at the school before I came home."

"I voted earlier today when the kids were in school. I took the day off today," Anne said as she served the spaghetti with meatballs.

"It's pasta night again," I said, disappointed.

Anne gave me a dirty look.

"Where are the kids?"

"Jack has a baseball game, Barbara is eating over her friend's house, and Robert is upstairs. He is coming down now." Anne said "Bobby, It is hard for my mom to do all the housework by herself. I took the day off just to help her."

I said, "Maybe you could find a job closer to home?"

Anne sat down for dinner. "I did. I found a job at the college."

"That sounds great. When do you start?"

"Next month," Anne said happily.

After dinner I helped Robert with his homework and went over the inventory books from the store. It was eleven o'clock when I turned on the television before I went to bed. Channel Two news predicted Adam Morley the winner in the New York State gubernatorial race.

34

I was doing some fall clean-up in the back yard when Jack asked me if he could borrow the keys to the LTD. "Sure, but be careful and be back by eight o'clock. Your mother and I are going out to eat with some friends."

"I will only be an hour. I have to pick up some books at the library," Jack said, grabbing the keys from my hand.

Jack was home from college. I got a good buy on the Ford LTD from a friend of Charlie's. I only paid five thousand for a ten-thousand-dollar car. I finished the cold iced tea Jack gave me and went into the house to take a shower.

We met Kevin and his wife, Mary, at Marko's Chinese Restaurant. We got to know Marko, a Chinese man, from having dinner at his restaurant many times. Marko served excellent food and he took good care of us. He also served exotic drinks. I introduced Kevin and Mary to Marko. We sat at a table in the back.

We talked for a while when I decided to ask Kevin, "Have you heard from your cousin Adam? It has been a few months since the election. I haven't heard from him at all."

"We keep in touch every now and then. I spoke to him last month. He is a busy man."

I nodded. "I bet he is."

"He mentioned Joey's name. He said that he is working on his pardon. It takes some time. There are a lot of legal ramifications. Have you visited Joey lately?"

I felt a pang of guilt. "No, I haven't seen him in years," I said, dipping my spareribs in duck sauce. The spareribs were a little burnt, just the way I liked them.

"I'll have another Blue Hawaiian," Kevin said, finishing his first drink.

I think Anne and Mary were getting bored with our conversation. They started to talk about the kids.

"Adam asked how you were doing, and he also asked about Maz. I told him that you and I keep in touch but I haven't talked to Maz since we were teenagers."

I said, "Maz got into trouble a little while back but he is doing well now. He is in homicide and is a second-grade detective. I don't really want to mention it but I think Adam had something to do with it."

We finished our dinner and I picked up the check.

As we were leaving I asked Kevin, "I know Adam has a office in midtown. Do you think he'd mind if I visit him one day?"

"I'm sure he wouldn't, Bobby."

35

It was a Wednesday night when I finished doing some paperwork and went to bed. I was sound asleep when the phone rang. I looked at the alarm clock. It was 3:20 in the morning. I answered the phone. It was a sergeant from the ninetieth precinct. "Is this Robert Lapchek?"

"Yes, this is he."

"You own a store at 183 Bedford Avenue?"

"Yes."

"Well, your building alarm was activated and it looks like someone broke in your back door. We disabled your alarm, but you have to come down and secure the premises and take a report."

"I will be there in less than an hour." I told Anne about break-in, and then got dressed and headed out to the store.

When I arrived there were two police officers in the store. One asked me if this was my store. I told him yes and showed him my identification. He told me to go over my inventory to see if anything was missing. The first place I went to was behind the front counter underneath the cash register. I hide some cash there, so I don't have to carry it home with me all the time. I couldn't find the cash. I told the officer that there was about five hundred dollars in cash. He asked me if any other merchandise was missing. I told him that some clothes were missing from a rack in the back.

"Some clothes?" he said. "I thought this was a grocery store. Fill out the report and make sure you secure the back door."

I asked him, "Are there any suspects?"

"No, there haven't been any other burglaries in the neighborhood. I will keep my eyes open. There will be somebody coming down in the morning to take fingerprints. Try not to touch the back door."

It was now six o'clock. There was no reason to go back home, so I decided to open the store early.

Charlie walked in the store and asked, "Bob, what happened?"

"Someone broke in last night and took the cash from underneath my register."

"I'm sorry to hear that," Charlie said.

I then told him, "The police said there weren't any break-ins around the neighborhood. Someone had to know I hid my cash underneath the register. "

Charlie said, "I don't know who would break in and take the money."

I was calming down when I told Charlie, "Go to work and try not to let anyone touch the back door."

I decided to give Maz a call. "Maz, how are you?"

"Good, Bobby, what's up?"

"Someone broke into my store last night. They took some cash I had on hand. The police were here. They did a fine job, but I was wondering if you could find out anything more?"

"I am real busy on a homicide case now. I have a good friend at the ninetieth precinct. I'll give him a call and see if he has any information."

I explained to Maz, "I just want to see if there were other burglaries in the neighborhood or if someone was targeting me. You know that Tony Russo was around . . ."

"Oh, by the way, I have good news, now that you mention Tony Russo. I spoke to Adam the other day and Joey's pardon finally went through. Joey will be a free man come Friday. We should all get together and celebrate," Maz said.

I was happy to hear the good news. "Well it's about time."

"I have more good news. You know that case I was working on when I was in the Cold Case Squad."

"Yes."

"I couldn't keep it off my mind. They gave the case to another detective but he didn't do much with it. Remember the pedophile that was living on City Island? My partner and I brought him in for a line-up. He is a skinny man in his fifties now and lives alone. The toll collector who had seen a person leaving the landfill picked him out of the line-up. The man really aged, but he was able to recognize him. After my partner and I interrogated him for an hour and a half, we also told him that we had an eyewitness, and he finally admitted to all three of the murders. It was funny how this guy never asked for a lawyer. I guessed he finally wanted to get caught. He won't get the death penalty, but the inmates don't like child molesters, if you know what I mean."

"Great job!"

"We'll all get together next week. I'll give you a call." Maz said as he hung up the phone.

I closed the store an hour early and decided to go home. It had been an exhausting day. I walked into the kitchen and there were two men in suits sitting down with Anne drinking a cup of coffee. My heart skipped a beat. I knew these guys were cops.

The heavyset one with his belly hanging over his belt asked me, "Robert, do you own a Ford LTD with the registration HTX-765?"

I was a little confused. "Yes, I do."

The officer said, "Like I explained to your wife, we are with the Federal Bureau of Investigation, and we believe that your car was stolen by an organization that are stealing automobiles all around the New York City area. These perps take the stolen cars to a garage in Queens, change the VIN numbers, and paint the cars different colors. Then they sell the cars on the open market. We believe the Mob is behind this.

I was stunned. "I knew the deal was too good to be true. What happens now?" I asked.

The fat cop said with a little grin on his face, "I guess you are out of luck. We have to take the car."

"You have to be kidding me! You mean I'm out of a car?"

"I'm sorry but there's nothing I can do."

I looked at Anne and we both shrugged our shoulders. Great, now I had no car.

I decided to give Adam a call about my car.

"Bobby, how the hell are you?" Adam said while I could hear him shuffle some papers in the background.

"Are you busy?" I said.

"No, and even if I was I still have time for you, Bobby. What's up?"

I told Adam about my stolen car.

"Maybe that character Tony Russo was part of the organization. I'll look into it but there isn't much you could do. The only alternative is to write the loss off on your taxes next year."

"Come on, Adam, write the loss off on my taxes? I will never get the money back?"

"That is the only thing you can do. The law is the law," Adam said. "Did you know that Joey is now a free man?"

"I know, Maz told me. That is great news."

"I went up to Greenville myself. I sat him down, looked him straight in his eyes, and whispered to him on how grateful I was for him taking the rap for me. I also pleaded with Joey not to get involved with that clown Tony Russo. I told him he was bad man. Joey promised me that he would stay away from him. Bobby, the four of us want to get together Saturday night at Peter Logan's. I reserved a back room for us. It will be like old times."

I told Adam, "I wouldn't miss it for the world."

36

As soon as I walked into Peter Logan's the hostess recognized me. "They are in the back room waiting for you."

Adam, Maz, and Joey were all standing in the back room with drinks in their hands. I went right over to Joey and embraced him. "Great to see you, Joey."

Joey grinned and said, "I see you have aged a little, Bobby. Some gray hair and a little belly."

Maz handed me a beer. "Three kids will do it to you. How does it feel to be a free man?"

"Fantastic. I can't thank Adam enough," Joey said.

"I think we should be thanking you," I told Joey.

"It was twenty-three long years in that prison," Joey said while Adam put his hand on Joey's shoulder.

"That first asshole judge sentenced you to fifteen years," Maz said angrily.

I could see the fire in Joey's eyes. "That's how much that fuckin prick judge and warden hated me. The warden charged me with assault a couple of times and made sure I did the extra time. I hope I never meet them in the street. But I promised Adam that I would be a good boy."

"Where are you staying?" I asked Joey as we all sat down at the table.

Joey put his arm around Adam. "Adam put me up in an apartment on the north side until I get myself on my feet. He even offered me a job in his office, but I got a job waiting tables at Ruggios, an Italian restaurant on Kent Avenue and North Fifth Street. The restaurant opened up after the Budweiser factory closed. A friend of mine offered me the job."

I didn't want to say anything, but I knew that Tony Russo hung out at that restaurant.

Maz raised his glass. "Lets drink to Joey being a free man and starting a new life!"

We all finished our drinks. The waiter came over and we ordered our steaks and more drinks.

Maz said, "Joey, remember when we were fourteen and you took your father's old Rambler? We all jumped in and went for a joy ride. Then the car got stuck in a ditch on Havenmeyer Street. I told you that I could lift the car by myself. I was doing pretty well for a while until my hands started to sweat and the car slipped. It felt like hours before you fuckers got that car off of my foot!"

"It took a while to find the old rusty jack," I had to remind Maz.

We all laughed

Adam said, "Bobby, remember when you were bragging that you could swim out to the buoy in the East River?"

I interrupted. "Come on, Adam that buoy was practically in the middle of the river."

"Joey and I had to jump in and drag you back to the pier."

The patrons outside the room could hear us laughing so loud.

It was Joey's turn. "Guys, remember the night that we tried stealing some beer from Mr. Diaz's store? Diaz end up chasing us into the south side . . ." Joey stopped and took a sip from his bourbon.

Adam, Maz and I all looked at each other and stopped ginning. We didn't know which way Joey was going with this. If he wanted us to feel sorry for him or tell him what a great man he was for taking the rap for the murder.

I quickly changed the subject. "Maz, you were telling me that you were working on a homicide."

"Yeah, that's right, Bobby. It happened over in Bay Ridge, Brooklyn. A man was found with a gunshot wound in his head. He was killed execution style. Looks like it may have been Mob related. There were receipts with baseball teams and names of horses on them. There were also receipts with amounts of money. There were no names on the receipts. No gun was found and we have no eyewitnesses. Looks like some kind of organized gambling."

Joey jumped in. "It was probably a friend that he had a bet with. I wouldn't look into that Mob hit or organized gambling too much."

"Yeah, you think so, Joey? You wouldn't have anything to do with it?" Maz asked, practically yelling at Joey.

Joey yelled back at Maz, "No fuckin way, Maz!"

The waiter brought out our steaks and another drink.

We all were quiet for a minute when I asked Maz, "Any news on the burglary at my store?"

Adam glanced at me. "Someone broke into your store, Bobby? What did they take?"

"About five hundred dollars in cash."

Maz finished chewing on his steak. "My buddy hasn't called me. I'll give him a call this week."

We finished our steaks then ordered some more rounds of drinks. It seemed like the old days down at the pier.

We stayed until the most of the patrons left the restaurant. There was no way I was able to drive home. Adam had his driver wait outside until we finished dinner. The poor guy waited for six hours. "Let me give you a ride home," Adam, said.

"No, I'm going to sleep over my parents' house tonight."

"Alright, let me give you a ride over there," Adam ordered.

I jumped into the limousine with him.

My Mother was waiting for me. I told her earlier in the day that I might spend the night there.

"How was your dinner with your friends, Robert?" She asked.

I told her about the dinner and how everyone was doing. Then I called Anne to tell her that I was spending the night over my parents' house.

"How is Dad doing?" I went into his room to see that he was sleeping and noticed the oxygen tank near his bed.

"The doctor put him on oxygen. He sleeps most of the day." Mom sounded worried.

"Come and stay with Anne and I. We will make room for the two of you," I told her.

"You know, Robert, I may have to take you up on that offer. Dad is getting harder to care for by myself," Mom said with a smile on her face.

"Good then, I'll make the arrangements this week."

I went over to the spare room and went to sleep before my head hit the pillow.

37

Two weeks had passed since I told my mother I would move her and my father to Staten Island. I planned to move them in a couple of weeks before the winter came.

The store was crowded for a Tuesday when Joey walked in. "Hey, Bobby, that was some night we had last month. I still have a hangover."

I told Joey, "Hey we should do it again soon."

"I didn't get a chance to ask you that night, how are your parents doing?"

I started to ring up Mr. Glinski's bill. "My dad isn't doing well. I plan on moving them in with me on Staten Island. Anne says she is fine with it. It is going to be a little tight, but we will get by."

Joey was now going through the daily newspaper and paying special attention to the sports section. "Bobby, do you like any of these horses running at Aqueduct today?" he asked as he handed me the newspaper with a couple of races circled.

I was stunned that Joey was actually telling me that he was into gambling. I just came out and said to him,

"Are you running numbers for that asshole Tony Russo? Joey, I don't want to see you go back to the joint again --"

"No, Bobby, I'm trying to start a little business on my own. I still have to make a living. The job at the Ruggios doesn't pay much."

I didn't know if Joey was bullshitting me. Just to please him, I said, "Give me twenty bucks on the number four horse in the fifth race to win. But if I find out you are working for Tony, I will personally throw you at of my store for good."

Joey grinned. "You can trust me, Bobby, and thanks for the business."

I watched Joey leave the store and get into a black Lincoln Continental. There was another person driving that I couldn't recognize. I quickly took down the license plate number. I gave Maz a call at work to see if he could run the plate. Another detective answered the phone and said Maz was out in the field. I left a message asking Maz to call me.

Charlie walked up front. "Was that Joey Bettino? He asked as he folded his arms. "I had dinner with my wife at Ruggios the last Saturday. He was sitting at a corner table with Tony Russo and two other men in suits. I overheard them talking. An older guy in his sixties with gray hair asked Joey how business was. Joey told him that business was great, and then I seen Joey hand the man a stack of bills. There must have been four to five thousand of dollars in that stack."

I told Charlie softly, "Joey is a good man. He just keeps getting mixed up with the wrong crowd . . ." Then I thought of something. The night we all got together,

Maz mentioned that he was working on a homicide. A man in Bay Ridge was found shot dead with racing forms receipts. Joey tried to put the shooting on the victim's friend. I wondered if Joey had anything to do with that murder. I knew I had to do something fast, but what? Joey was getting deeper and deeper into trouble again.

38

I closed the store around six o'clock. The traffic on the Brooklyn-Queens Expressway was unbelievable for a Tuesday evening. I heard on the radio that there was an eight-wheel tractor-trailer that overturned by the Brooklyn-Queens Tunnel exit a mile from where I was stopped in traffic. A good hour had gone by before traffic started to move. They must have towed the truck because there were no sign of a tractor-trailer where the accident had taken place. It's funny because you could sit in traffic for a long time and not know why.

As soon as I passed the tunnel exit I looked in my rear view mirror and saw the exact same Chevy that the mystery man got into the time I chased him on Bedford Avenue. I kept the same speed on my rental Buick Regal. For the next couple of miles the car was still behind me. I started to slow down but he kept on slowing down his car when I did. I couldn't make out the plate number. I decided to go faster to try and loose him. The mystery man's car started to go faster. I then weaved in and out of traffic. The car was still keeping pace with my car. I was getting a little nervous now. There were no shoulders on the highway. The Verazzano-Narrows Bridge was approaching. I could stop the car on the bridge and get a good look at the man but that would be too dangerous. The tolls were coming up. There seemed to be a million toll lanes by the bridge. I was hoping the man wouldn't choose the same toll lane as mine. I decided I would get of the Bay Street exit right after the tolls. This way I could stop and take a look at who this mystery man was if he was still following me.

I was now on Bay Street heading down by the water. The car was still behind me. Now there were streetlights on every other block. Bay Street was a two-lane street both in west and east directions. There were parked cars on each side, which really made the street one-lane in each direction.

There was a traffic light by Fingerboard Road. The light turned red. I waited until the man pulled his Chevy behind the Ford Bronco that was behind me. I opened my driver's door and started to walk to the Chevy. The next thing I saw was the man turning his head away from me and the Chevy moving across the double yellow lines, picking up speed and heading right towards me. I had to jump onto the Ford Bronco's hood to avoid the being struck by the car. I rolled off the Bronco's hood onto the street. The man in the Bronco rushed over and asked me if I was all right. I stood up. I was a little woozy but didn't have any injuries. I asked the man, "Did you get a look at the guy in the Chevy or take down the plate number?"

"Man, It happened so fast that I couldn't get a good look at him."

I asked him, "Which direction did he go?"

"He went west on Bay Street. You're not going after

him, are you? He practically tried to run you over. Do you want me to call the police?"

"No, if you couldn't see the plate number there is no sense making a report. Thank you . . . I think I am going to go home now."

I shook his hand and got into my car. I drove down Bay Street for a while but didn't see any sign of the mystery man's car.

When I arrived home, Anne barked, "Where the hell were you? We had dinner without you. The kids were hungry."

I sat down and started to eat what was left of the lasagna. "I was sitting in traffic for two hours. There was a tractor-trailer on the BQE that overturned. It should have been on the news." I finished my dinner, took a nice hot shower, watched a little television, and went to bed wondering, *who is the mystery man and why is he after me?*

39

I was sound asleep when I awoke to the noise of the garbage trucks outside of my house. I looked at the clock. It was 4:30 in the morning. It seemed like there was something wrong. I glanced over at Anne's side of the bed and she was not there. I guessed she was in the kitchen making coffee. I went into the kitchen and she was not there. Veronica was also up. I asked her, "Did you see Anne?"

"No, and Jack is not in his bed either." I could see the fear on Veronica's face. "Maybe someone took them," she said.

I told her in a firm voice. "No, they probably went somewhere --"

Just then the phone rang. It was Jack. "Dad, you better come over here."

"Where?"

"There has been an accident. A fire started in Grandma and Grandpa's apartment. They are in pretty bad shape."

I turned white. "I'll be right over, son. Is your mother with you?"

Jack replied, "Yes, she is okay."

A million thoughts were going through my mind. I told Veronica that Anne and Jack were safe and that there was fire at the store. That's where they went. They didn't want to wake us.

I was looking all over for the keys to the Buick when I realized that Jack and Anne must have taken it. I ran over to Sean's house. I felt bad knocking on his door early in the morning. "Sean, there has been an accident with my parents. Can I borrow your car to go over to their house?"

"Absolutely, Bobby, but you have to let me drive you there. It looks like you are in no shape to drive. What happened?"

My hands were now trembling. "I'll tell you on the ride over to Greenpoint."

I told Sean everything that Jack had told me. That was the only conversation in the car. The hour ride to Greenpoint seemed like three hours.

We approached North Fifth Street and Bedford Avenue. Sean couldn't drive any further. The street was blocked from North Fifth Street to North Seventh Street with fire trucks. I ran out of the car straight to the apartment building. It was hectic all over. There was a policeman and yellow tape stopping all pedestrian traffic on the corner of North Seventh and Bedford Avenue. I told the policeman, "I am the owner of the building." The officer let me through.

Charlie came running over. "Bobby, I'm sorry to hear about your parents."

I started to turn pale again. "What happened to my parents, Charlie?"

There was a few seconds of silence. I knew that

I didn't want to hear the next words to come out of Charlie's mouth. "Your dad passed away in the fire. And your mother died on the way to Our Lady Of Mercy. I am sorry, Bobby."

I could feel my knees buckling. I sat down on the curb and started to cry. Jack came over and put his arms around me. I asked him, "Where is your mother? Is she okay?"

"Mom is fine. She is in the ambulance getting oxygen. She fainted when she heard the news."

There were so many ambulances around; it took me a while to find her. We hugged each other and started crying. I asked Anne, "How did it happen?"

Anne wiped her tears away. "I am not sure. All I know is that the fireman told me that the fire started in the second floor hallway."

I started to walk away.

"Where are you going, Robert?" Anne asked.

"I'm going to find someone that knows how this happened."

A fireman with a jacket that read Deputy Chief Branigan was ordering other fireman around. I approached him. "Sir, my parents passed away in the fire. Can you please tell me what happened?"

Deputy Chief Branigan took me aside. "First, my condolences regarding your parents. Looks like the fire started in the second floor hallway. I don't exactly know how, probably from some faulty wiring in the ceiling. We have to wait until the fire marshal arrives to investigate the cause. There was a lot of smoke in the apartment, and because your father was bed-ridden he passed away from smoke inhalation. Your mother had plenty of time to get out alive by the fire escape, but she didn't want to leave your father. She couldn't carry him by herself. One saving grace was that the fire was mainly contained to your parents' apartment and there were no other fatalities. There was little damage to your store on the first floor. As soon as I hear word from the fire marshal I'll let you know what exactly caused the fire."

I shook the Chief's hand. "Thank you very much for all your help."

The fire was completely out. The firemen were packing up their fire trucks. I went back to Anne who was still in the ambulance.

"We are taking your wife to Our Lady of Mercy for precautionary reasons. She may have hit hear head on the ground when she fainted. Do you want to ride in the ambulance with her?" The paramedic asked me as he started to close the ambulance door.

"No, I am alright," Anne, pleaded with the paramedic.

"I will go with you. The paramedics are concerned. I have to find Sean. He drove me over here from Staten Island. I will tell Jack to take the car back home, he is tired," I told Anne.

"Go ahead, my partner and I will wait for you," the paramedic said.

There was still a crowd in the street; everyone was talking about the fire. Some were my regular customers from the store asking how my parents were. I told them that they had perished in the fire. They were all upset. I finally found Sean. "The asshole cop wouldn't let me through. I kept telling him that I was with you. How are your parents?"

"They didn't make it. My father died in the fire and my mother passed away on the way to the hospital."

Sean put his arm around my shoulder. "I am really sorry, Bobby."

"I am going with Anne in the ambulance to Our Lady Of Mercy. She is fine but the paramedics want her to get checked out. Can you meet me there?"

Sean said, "Sure Bobby. I'll follow the ambulance on the way to the hospital."

Anne and I didn't say much on the way there. We still had tears in our eyes. The ambulance arrived at Our Lady Of Mercy Hospital. I went with Anne to the emergency room. There were three firemen being treated for smoke inhalation. All of them expressed their condolences for the loss of my parents.

Anne was treated very quickly.

A woman who was nicely dressed approached us. "Mr. and Mrs. Lapchek, I am sorry for your loss. I am Mrs. Smith, the hospital administrator. I know it is a bad time but I need one of you to identify your parents."

I told Anne, "I will go. I need to see them."

Mrs. Smith led the way to the morgue. It was a cold and damp place down three flights in the sub-basement. There was a man dressed in all white that opened two small doors and pulled out two stretchers that my mother and father laid on. The man pulled back the sheets to make sure that I acknowledged the two bodies were my parents. It was the hardest thing I had to do in my life. I nodded my head yes and left the room.

Mrs. Smith followed me. "Thank you, Mr. Lapchek, I know that was a hard thing to do."

I walked back upstairs to Anne. Sean and Anne were standing near the exit of the hospital. I told them weakly, "Let's go home."

40

It was twelve o'clock in the afternoon when we arrived home. I called up Kolinsky's Funeral Polar to make funeral arrangements. Kolinsky's was located directly across the street from Our Lady of Help Church. I wanted the viewing of my parents to be for only one day. Friday was the earliest day the funeral parlor had available. There would be two viewings on Friday, one in the afternoon and the other in the evening. The funeral would follow the next day on Saturday.

I was so exhausted. I told the kids that I was going to bed, and if anyone called I would talk to them tomorrow. I slept from three o'clock in the afternoon on Wednesday to ten o'clock in the morning on Thursday.

Everyone was calling to send their condolences and inquire about the funeral arrangements. One call I received was from Deputy Chief Branigan. "How are you feeling, Bobby? I received the results on the cause of the fire from the lab. It looks like there was some kind of accelerant used."

I was in shock. "You mean there was no faulty wiring in the ceiling?"

"No, the lab report is usually accurate. We are not sure what accelerant was used. It may have been plain old gasoline. We are ruling it as arson."

Someone started the fire. But who?

The funeral parlor was packed. There was a line that extended out the door. The flower arrangements took up half the room. I never shook so many hands and kissed so many people before.

Joey and Maz came in the evening.

"Bobby, I am so sorry. If there is anything that I can do just let me know. I talked to Adam. He couldn't make it tonight but he will be at the funeral tomorrow," Maz said as he put his arms around me.

I whispered to Maz and Joey, "We will talk tomorrow after the funeral."

"Sure, Bobby," Maz said as he shook my hand.

The rest of the night went the same way, shaking hands and thanking everyone for their condolences.

The funeral was even more crowded then the wake. Every pew was filled and people were standing outside the church to pay their respects. It was a beautiful mass. I stood at the altar to say the eulogy about what wonderful human beings my parents were. Outside the church there must have been a hundred people. The press was also there taking pictures. I had my parents buried at Saint John's Cemetery in Queens. The funeral procession was five city blocks long. We even had a police escort. Maz probably had it arranged. Father Mulligan from Our Lady Of Help said a few prayers as we laid my parents to rest. It was the saddest time in my life.

"The Lapchek family would like to thank everyone for coming. They would like everyone to attend a thank-you dinner at the American Polish Hall in Greenpoint." I'd asked the funeral director to say this after the cemetery.

I was surprised to see most of the people from the cemetery come back to the Polish Hall. There were mostly immediate family and close friends at the hall. Adam came over and embraced me. "Sorry I missed the wake the last night. Your parents were the nicest people. It was a shame that they had to die that way."

Joey and Maz walked over to join us. I said, "Let's grab a few beers and go into the backyard." There was a small yard with a little grass in the back of the hall. Patrons went there to have a cigarette.

I thanked Maz. "That was some police escort. We flew to the cemetery."

Maz chugged down his beer. "It was the least that I could have done."

Joey lit a cigarette.

"When did you start smoking?" I asked.

"I picked it up in the joint," Joey said, offering me a cigarette.

"Get the hell out of here," I told him and we both laughed. It was the first laugh I had in a while.

"Bobby, I heard that the fire was caused by some faulty wiring in the walls. Is that true?" Adam asked.

"Funny you ask, Adam. I got a call from Chief Branigan on Thursday. He received the report from the lab. The report said that the cause was not by faulty wiring but done by an accelerant." I could hear the anger in my voice. "The lab couldn't pinpoint what kind of accelerant it was but he thinks it might have been gasoline."

"Are you kidding me?" Maz said. "That means it was done deliberately."

Joey, Maz, and Adam all stood motionless.

Maz then started to speak after a long silence. "Do you think it was Tony Russo? You were telling me that you had words with him."

"It's a possibility. But I don't think he would stoop that low. I have another story to tell you. There has been this man that's been following me around for sometime --"

Maz jumped in. "Is that the same man you told me that you saw at Frank's Pizzeria? That was a long time ago."

"Well, he is back." I told them about the time I saw the man across the street staring at the grocery store. I also told them about the time before the fire when the asshole in the car followed me on the BQE and almost killed me by trying to run me over.

Adam looked concerned. "This sounds serious."

I agreed. "I don't need this asshole coming after my family."

Maz slammed his empty beer into the receptacle. "That's it, I am pulling myself off all my cases to find out who this dick is."

Adam was deep in thought. "Easy, Maz. This is what we are going to do. I am going to talk to the feds and lean on the Masimino Family. I'll put an injunction on their shipping industry. Maybe this will get Tony Russo or whoever is responsible to come out. We can't let Bobby and his family worrying about this prick. We also have to get some protection for them."

I was feeling better already. "Thanks," I said to Adam.

"Adam, I don't think that Tony Russo had anything to do with this," Joey said.

I was so mad at Joey. "Is that right, Joey? Anyway, why are you still hanging around him? You've been seen talking with him at Ruggios almost every night. The other day you came into the store asking if I wanted to play the horses. To top it all off, there's the case Maz is working on where the police found a man shot in the head with racing form receipts. You told Maz that Tony Russo had nothing to do with that murder also. You're in trouble again. Adam had to pull a few strings to get you out of jail . . ."

Adam stared at Joey. "Is that true, Joey?"

Joey looked at the ground. "Yes, Adam, it's true. But I still believe Tony had nothing to do with Bobby's parents' death." Joey slowly turned his head down again and walked back into the hall.

We went into the hall to look for Joey, but there was no sign of him.

41

It had been a few months since my parents passed away, and there wasn't a day that I didn't think about them. My parents left the store and the apartment building to my two sisters and me. I opened the store last month. It took some time for the contractors to renovate my parents' apartment. The ceiling in the store had to be fixed. The insurance covered most of the renovations. The contractors did an excellent job, and the place looked like new.

Charlie walked in the store ten minutes after I opened up. "Bob, I brought you the paper and a cup of coffee. Look at the front-page headline. Your friend Adam Morley is doing some job."

I grabbed the *New York Times* that Charlie handed me. The front-page headline read HEAD OF MASAMINO FAMILY INDICTED FOR MURDER.

"Wow, I guess Adam was not kidding around," I said.

Charlie and I smiled at each other as I sipped my coffee. There was a huge picture on the front page of Leo Allesio, the head of the family, in handcuffs. I turned the page and read on. The article explained how the feds shut down a couple of the shipping companies that belonged to the Mob. The article further stated that the writer was perplexed as to why the feds were hitting the Mob so hard at this particular time. There were a few names of others arrested, but Tony Russo wasn't one of them.

I was anxious to find out more. I finished my coffee and decided to give Maz a call. He was yawning when he answered the phone. "Maz, you still sleeping?"

"Yeah, but I have to get up to work anyway. How have you been? Is everything quiet?"

"Everything is good. I opened the store back up. It took a few months for the renovations to the building. I've seen many police cars go by my house at all hours of the day. Did you have anything to with that?"

Maz hesitated then said, "No, I think it was Adam who put the word in."

I looked at the paper again. "Maz, were you involved with the feds that arrested the Masimino family?"

Maz yawned again. "Sorry, Bobby, I was working late last night. Yes, Adam has my team and I working jointly with the feds on the case. Our team went undercover to get the indictment on Leo Allesio."

"I didn't see Tony Russo's name in the paper . . ." Old man Glinski, who wanted to know the price of milk, interrupted me. "Two-fifty!" I yelled in his ear.

"We can't find Russo. Maybe Joey told him that we were after him, or maybe Joey was right that he wasn't involved with your parent's apartment. In fact, we interrogated Leo for a while regarding the arson and Leo seems pretty content that he or anyone of his stooges knew anything about the fire. We also have been going into the south side knocking a few heads around looking for your boy Juan, but no one has admitted seeing him. I do have a small lead on Juan. My partner and I have been visiting every bodega in the south side. One of the bodega owners said that two men came into his store to buy cigarettes. One of the men does fit Juan's description a little. It has been so many years I don't think I could even recognize him. But he did hear the other man call him Juan. There was another thing the bodega owner said. There were two other men in the store asking for Juan. Both men were white. One was skinny with receding black hair and the other was small and chubby with black hair. They left in a black Lincoln Continental."

I realized whom the owner was describing. "Maz, that sounds like Joey and Tony Russo. Joey was in the store the other day and I seen him leave in a black Lincoln Continental. I hope those two don't do any thing stupid."

"I'm still going to look further into it. We will probably set up an undercover in the store. I'll let you know as soon as I find out anything."

I hung up the phone after I thanked Maz.

42

I heard the doorbell ring. It was Sean. "Nice warm day for a Saturday in March. Is anybody else home?"

I invited Sean in. "No, Jack and Barbara are away at college. Anne took Robert to the movies and then out to eat with her mother." I handed Sean a beer from the refrigerator.

Sean took a sip; he looked like he had something on his mind. "How has everyone been holding up since your parents passed away? Did the police catch the sons of bitches that set the fire?"

"No, but I know they are still working on it."

"That's right, you're good friends with the governor."

"Adam has been putting all lot of pressure on the Mob. We think that one of their soldiers named Tony Russo had a hand in the arson."

Sean said, "Tony doesn't seem like the type of man to do something as horrible as that."

I was surprised to hear that out of Sean. "I didn't know that you were that good friends with Tony Russo." I began to wonder if Sean was part of the Masimino family.

"I know you have something on your mind, Sean. What is it?"

"Bobby, it is a huge hit."

I jumped back in my chair. "Come on, Sean, don't you ever stop?"

Sean moved closer to me. "No, Bobby, there is about ten of us. We are going to hijack some payroll trucks at the airport. They carry four to five million dollars on a bad day. There are some workers on the inside in on it. We have planned this out for a long time. It's a guarantee not to get caught. Are you in? You can retire for the rest of your life."

He made it sound so good I almost had to say yes. "I can't take the chance, Sean. I have three kids with two in college and one going soon." I gave Sean another beer.

"Bobby, this is a once in a lifetime opportunity. You'll be sorry if you say no."

I hesitated for a second and said, "No thanks, Sean."

Now he had put me in another predicament. *Should I rat out on him or not?*

43

I decided to take a vacation with Anne. With the events that we'd been through the past year we deserved it. I closed the store for two weeks. It was the middle of July and many of the customers were also on vacation, so it wouldn't hurt that much in the pocket. We were going to visit Tom and Lori in Florida. Tom had retired from the police department two years ago. He sold his house in Long Island and moved into a modest three-bedroom home with an in-ground pool in a quiet town called New Port Richey.

Lori and Tom met us at Tampa International Airport. It was the first time I was on a plane, and the flight was so bumpy I thought it would be my last.

New Port Richey was about forty miles north of Tampa. On the way from the airport Tom showed us the area. There were mostly developments, with about fifty to sixty homes in each community. Some of the communities had enormous pools along with tennis courts and a golf course. The golf courses were beautiful. I always wanted to take up the sport.

Tom said as he was pointing at some homes that were

under construction, "Are you two looking to move down here? It is a beautiful area. There is still plenty of land here. The developers sell the land in quarter-acre lots. A basic lot runs around ten thousand dollars, and if you want a house built it costs about eighty thousand dollars."

I was amazed. "That is cheap. You couldn't buy a shed for that price in Staten Island. But Anne and I have to wait for the kids to be living on their own before we move to Florida."

Tom glanced back at me. "Bobby, you could buy a lot and not build on it until you are ready to make the move. We'll go around the area tomorrow and look at more land."

After we settled in at Tom's, Anne and Lori went outside on the lanai, the cement patio next to the pool. Tom and I took a seat on the couch in the living room.

"Sorry to hear about your parents," Tom said, handing me a beer. "How is my partner doing? I only get to talk to him about once a month being down here."

"I don't know if Maz told you that he joined a special task force with the NYPD working jointly with the FBI. They just got Leo Allesio indicted on murder and racketeering charges. We think Tony Russo, who is a member of the family, might have something to do with my parents' deaths."

Tom was surprised. "The fire was an arson job? Maz never told me. So you think this guy Tony Russo had something to do with it?"

Tom brought me over another beer. "There is another man I seen following me around. This man goes way back to our teenage years. It's a long story. He followed me home one day and when I got out of my car to approach him he nearly ran me over. To this day I still don't know what this man looks like. He may be a man from an incident that happened with Maz and I when we were teenagers. Nobody else knows the story except Joey, Adam, Maz, and myself."

"Since you were teenagers! That was a long time ago. It must have been serious. What happened?"

I said, "I'd rather not get into it. We swore to each other that we would never tell anyone on what happened that summer night."

Tom and I finished the two six-packs in the refrigerator and went to bed.

The next day, Tom showed Anne and I some homes. We then traveled to Tampa. There were some beautiful homes right on the bay, but the asking price was too high for us. We had lunch at a seafood restaurant on the bay called Mack's Seafood Shack.

"Bobby, you can open a nice restaurant like this down here. The area is prettier than the north side, wouldn't you say? And the economy keeps growing and growing," Tom said as he was staring out the window onto the bay. The fishing boats were heading in to the harbor after a long day of work.

"Yeah, Tom, it sounds like a great idea." I picked up the check and we headed back to New Port Richey.

"Bobby, I want to show you some land near my house. Pretty inexpensive."

The land was in a community that the builder was starting to develop. There were only two homes that were already built. The lots that bordered the woods went for a little more money. Anne and I fell in love with a lot that was in a cul-de-sac with woods in the back. We talked to the builder.

"I will sell you that lot for twelve thousand dollars. Those lots normally go for fifteen thousand. I usually build a home on the lot right away, but if you want to wait a while to build that would be fine with me."

I looked at Anne and we both nodded in agreement. "It sounds like a great deal. I'll send you a check as soon as I get back to New York."

We went back to Tom's house to celebrate. I bought a bottle of champagne on the way. Tom turned on the television as I made a toast to our new purchase. Breaking news came on the television: The FBI had made a number of arrests at JFK airport. Eight men were arrested for attempting to hijack two payroll trucks that belonged to Sky Airlines. One FBI agent was injured in an exchange of gunfire. There were no other injuries. Two of the perpetrators were members of the Masamino family. The newscaster read all the names and Sean's was one.

"Sean Flynn—he lives down our block!" Anne said. "He came over to our house a few times . . . Bob is a good friend of his . . ."

I made sure that I sounded surprised. "Holy Shit! Please excuse my language. I never knew that Sean . . . Well, you never know, do you?"

I remembered that Sean mentioned he knew Tony Russo. Tony was not one of the names broadcast. I was kind of relived in a way.

I said to Tom, "I wonder if Maz was involved with the arrests. I told you that he was working the FBI. He must be busy now. I will give him a call when I get back to New York."

Tom raised his champagne glass. "That's my partner, always doing a great job."

One thing I knew, I wouldn't be seeing Sean for a long time.

44

When I went back to work the next week I decided to give Maz a call. Everything should have calmed down by now. "Maz, what's up?"

"Bobby, I been trying to call you at work last week. There was no answer. Are you all right? Did anything happen?" Max sounded concerned.

"I was visiting your old partner Tom down in sunny Florida for a week. He and Lori have a beautiful home. You wouldn't believe the prices on homes and land down there. I purchased land in an upcoming community for only twelve thousand dollars. You should go down and look around."

Maz said, "Sounds great, but the fuckin job took so many vacation days away the time I got jammed up, it'll be two years the next time I get time off."

I said, "When I was down there a special report came over the television that there was an attempted big heist at JFK airport. Were you in on the case?"

"Yeah, the feds and us were sitting on that case for a long time. We had two undercover agents planted on the inside."

I thought, *that is why eight people were arrested and not the ten Sean had originally said.* I told Maz, "One of the men arrested was my good friend, Sean Flynn. You might have met him one time"

Maz was shocked. "No shit! He wasn't one of the big players, but he is still going away for along time. Sorry to hear that, Bobby. On the other hand, I have good news to tell you. I came upon an important lead in your parents' case. I don't want to talk about it over the phone. My partner and I will be there in a couple of hours."

Sure enough, Maz and his partner walk into the store two hours later.

"Bobby, this is my partner, Phil. He works with me on the Federal Joint Task Force."

Phil extended his hand. "Glad to meet you, Bobby. Maz has told me a lot about you."

"Well, I have a lot to tell you about Maz." We all laughed.

"So, you've been down Florida visiting my ex-partner. How is he doing?" Maz asked with a smile.

As I rang up Mr. Glinski's grocery bill, I told Maz, "Lori and Tom are doing very well. Looks like retired life agrees with Tom. The weather down there is beautiful and the homes are --" Just then, the phone rang.

"Bobby, how the hell have you been?"

I didn't recognize the voice on the other end right away. "Joey, is that you?"

"That's right, this is your old friend Joey. Bobby, I am sorry that I left your parents' funeral without saying good-bye. You know that I have a bad temper. Anyway your worries are soon to be over with. Tony and I are going to take care of everything."

I was confused. "What do you mean, Joey, take care of everything?"

"You will see." Joey hung up the phone.

I turned to Maz. "That was Joey on the phone . . . He sounded serious, like he was going to do something. He said that he was going to take care of my troubles."

Maz yelled, "That's why I was calling you last week! Phil and I staked out the bodega on Bedford Avenue. It was the same bodega the man recognized Juan. Juan wasn't there but the owner pointed out the man that hangs out with him. Word on the street is that Juan was in Puerto Rico for a while and just got back to the States about the same time the arson happened. Phil and I followed this guy for three blocks. He ended up going into a rundown apartment building at 1135 Bedford Avenue over in the south side. We waited for about three hours but there was no sign of Juan so we left. Our intentions were to go back to stake out the apartment again, but we got too busy with the airport case. We better get over there quickly. Did Joey mention if he was on his way over there?"

"No, basically all he said that he was going to take care of everything and that I didn't have to worry anymore."

Maz yelled, "We have to find Juan before Joey finds him!"

Maz and Phil ran out the door. I froze for a second then jumped over the counter nearly knocking down Mr. Glinski who was walking out the door. I yelled to Charlie who was walking up front to see what the commotion was about. "Take over the register, I have to go somewhere!"

I opened Maz's unmarked Chevy Impala rear door

and jumped into the back seat. The car was parked in front of the store at a bus stop. We were getting dirty looks from people waiting for the bus. Phil was driving.

Maz turned his head towards me. "Where in the hell do you think you are going? Phil, stop the car and let him out."

My heart was pounding. "No way, Maz, I'm coming."

Phil said, "We have no time to stop. Maz you better radio that we have a pick-up of a man with a possible gun at 1135 Bedford Avenue. Bobby, you are in for the ride of your life?"

Phil quickly made a U-turn and headed south on Bedford Avenue towards the south side and 1135 Bedford Avenue. Phil drove past North Sixth Street and then North Fifth Street. Maz pointed out, "Phil, the cars up there are not moving. It looks like there is an accident up ahead at North Second Street. Looks like there is a city bus involved." Phil quickly made a right hand turn onto North Fourth Street. We were now going westbound. The car seemed like it was on two wheels. But North Fourth Street was a one-way street eastbound, and as soon as we turned there was another car coming right for us. There were parked cars on each side of the street and no way for us to get by. Phil turned onto a driveway and then made a quick left turn. We were now driving on the sidewalk. There were front stoops sticking out on the right side and some trees on the left. Now I saw a man walking his dog and two kids playing hopscotch fifty yards ahead of us. Sweat was pouring down my face. Phil then turned into another driveway and back into the street avoiding the pedestrians. He made a left onto Roebling Avenue. We were now safe. Roebling was a two-way Avenue.

I was out of breath when I said, "We don't even know if Juan committed the arson."

Maz looked at Phil. "No, we don't have any evidence; but if you put two and two together it doesn't take a rocket scientist to know that he did it."

Phil made a right hand turn from Broad Street. We were now on Bedford Avenue on the south side. I could see the needle on the speedometer at 100 miles per hour. Two cars were stopped at a red light on South Third Street in front of our car. Phil decided to turn the car across the double yellow line and into the opposite lane of traffic around the two stopped cars. There was a minivan coming straight at us. The driver of the van jammed on his brakes as our car swayed between the van and the first car stopped at the light, narrowly missing another car going eastbound on South Third Street.

Phil slammed on the brakes between South Eighth and South Ninth Streets in front of 1135 Bedford Avenue. It was an old rundown apartment building that consisted of four floors.

Maz turned and pointed his finger at me. "Bobby, you stay the fuck in the car. I don't need a civilian causality."

I pleased Maz by saying, "Sure, Maz." But curiosity got the best of me. I waited about half a minute and decided to follow Maz and Phil into the building. As soon as I entered the building I could smell the stench of piss in the hallways. I walked up to the first floor. Everybody had his or her front doors closed. No one wanted to get involved. One person opened her front door slightly to peek out and see what was going on. She quickly shut the door when she saw me.

I walked up to the second floor; there was no sign of

Phil and Maz. I then heard, "Holy shit!" It was Maz. I ran up the third flight of stairs and saw two men shot on the living room floor. One of the men was the same one that was following me over the years. He looked like Juan but I still wasn't sure.

"Are they dead?" Maz asked Phil as he was checking them for a pulse.

"Dead as a rat's ass," Phil said, standing up at looking at me.

"*I told you to stay the fuck in the car!*" I'd never heard Maz yell at me so loud since I knew him.

Both the man and his amigo had execution-style bullet wounds to their heads. Maz looked out the kitchen window in the rear of the apartment. "No sign of anyone back here."

I asked Maz nervously, "Do you think, Russo and Joey had something to with this?"

Maz didn't say anything. He just gave me a look like, who else could have committed the murders?

Phil said, "This other guy is the same guy we followed a couple of weeks ago."

Maz went into a storage area near the kitchen. "Phil, take a look at this." Maz pointed out to two gasoline containers that were in a small closet.

"Call this in," Phil said.

Maz spoke into the radio. "Slow it down at 1135 Bedford Avenue. Everything is under control. There are two men shot. The perps have fled the scene. I have no direction of flight and no description of the perps at this time."

Two minutes later four other officers along with a sergeant entered the apartment. Maz started telling the sergeant what happened. The sergeant nodded to me and asked Maz, "Who is that?" Maz told the sergeant I'm a civilian ride-along. The sergeant ordered me out and told one officer to call the Crime Scene Unit. ·

I left the building and decided to walk back to the store knowing Maz would be busy for a while and wondering where the fuck Joey and Tony Russo were.

I went home, had dinner, and put the television on, not saying a word to Anne about what happened. The headline story was about the two murders in the Greenpoint section of Brooklyn. Two Hispanic men were shot execution-style in a brownstone at 1135 Bedford Avenue. The police did not release the identity of the victims. The motive was uncertain. However, the police were looking for two men wanted in the shootings. Joey Bettino a white, thin man approximately five foot nine with black hair. The other was Tony Russo a white man, stocky, approximately five foot six with black receding hair. "These men are armed and dangerous. Do not take any action. Call the police." Then the news station showed mug shots of Joey and Tony. I was wondering how the police knew it was them. The news reporter said there was an eyewitness who'd seen the two men leave the building.

I didn't tell anyone. I tried to fall asleep but tossed and turned all night feeling like the murders were my fault.

45

I hadn't heard any news on the whereabouts of Joey and Tony for three days. I didn't even hear from Maz.

I was ringing up some customers at the register when I heard police sirens go by. Then I heard the sound of a helicopter above us. Charlie walked to the front of the store. "Bob, did you hear all the sirens and the helicopter?"

Mr. Daly, one of my steady customers, came into the store and said, "There must be something going on down by North Seventh and Kent Avenue. There are about ten police cars there."

I turned up my radio and switched the station from a music station to WABC, a news station. The news reporter said that the police had two men, Joey Bettino and Tony Russo, wanted for two homicides held up in an abandoned building at 546 North Seventh Street. I turned to Charlie. "Let's close the store for a while."

It was lunchtime so I closed the store and we quickly headed to 546 North Seventh Street. We couldn't go any further than the corner of Kent Avenue on North Seventh Street. There was a large crowd and television reporters everywhere. The police had the block taped off. There were three other buildings on each side of the street before the East River. 546 North Seventh Street was one of a few buildings that were not yet renovated. I looked around and saw Maz standing by an unmarked police car. I yelled to him, but he couldn't hear me. I tried calling his name again.

He finally looked around and saw me. He walked over. "It's not good, Bobby. Joey and Tony Russo are held up on the second floor. They started shooting and won't come down. We called his brother Johnny to talk to him; he is on his way."

"You should also give Adam a call. Maybe he can talk some sense to him."

Maz stared at me for a second. "Sounds like a good idea. Why don't you come with me?"

I walked with Maz to the unmarked police car. Maz handed me a bullhorn and asked me, "Here, Bobby, maybe you could talk to Joey? He is by the second floor window on the left side of the building."

My hands were trembling as Maz gave me the bullhorn. Maz went into the car to call Adam. I put the bullhorn to my mouth. "Joey, this is Bobby . . . can you please come down? I don't want to see you get hurt. There is no way of getting out of here."

There was no answer from the apartment building.

Maz jumped out of the car. "Adam is on his way. He is in the city and should be here in about fifteen minutes. The police are giving him an escort."

Joey's brother Johnny arrived. It had been a couple of years since I last saw him. Maz handed Johnny the bullhorn. "Try and talk some sense into your brother."

"It's your bro, Johnny. Joey, please listen to me. I don't want to see my brother go down like this. I am coming in after you."

Again there was no answer from the second floor window. Johnny put the bullhorn down. Maz stepped in front of him. "Sorry, Johnny, I can't let you go in there."

"Please, he is my brother! I don't want to see him get hurt."

Phil came over and stood next to Maz. "Johnny, we won't let you go in. Joey is acting crazy. He may take his own brother hostage."

We all heard police sirens in the background. There were two police cars and a black Lincoln trying to get through the crowd. The Lincoln car door opened and Adam exited the passenger side. He walked right over to us and immediately grabbed the bullhorn. "Joey, this is Adam. If you are not coming out I am coming in." No one was going to stop Adam from going in after Joey.

As soon as he walked into the front door a voice came from the window. "Alright, we are going to surrender. Adam, don't come in." It was Joey's voice.

Everyone stopped talking. There was dead silence among the crowd. Adam walked back towards us. We waited. Five minutes went by. Neither Joey nor Tony walked through the front door. Just as I said to Maz, "What the fuck do we do now?" Joey started walking through the front door.

A police captain that was standing four feet from us spoke into his bullhorn. "Put your hands up where I can see them."

Joey and Tony put their hands above their heads. Joey was walking in front of Tony. What happened next was unbelievable. Tony pushed Joey in the back. Joey fell to the ground. Tony put his right hand into his waistband. Everybody took cover. Tony pulled out a semi-automatic pistol, and before he could fire his first shot, there was gunfire everywhere from the police. Tony didn't stand a chance. There was blood gushing out from bullet holes all over Tony's body. Everyone watched in shock.

Joey remained on the ground with his hands over his head. Maz, Phil, and two other police officers started slowly walking towards Joey and Tony with their firearms out. Maz yelled to Joey who was still on the ground, "Buddy, are you alright?"

Joey started to get up. "Yeah, I'm okay."

Maz grabbed Joey by the shirt and helped him up with one hand with his gun still in the other. "Joey, put your hands behind your back. I have to cuff you."

Joey obliged. Maz then began to search Joey for any weapons. There were none. Maz walked Joey to where Adam, Johnny, and I were standing. Johnny began to cry and put his arms around Joey.

Maz asked, "Why, Joey? We were close to arresting those two assholes."

Joey just stared at Maz and then said, "They had it coming. Anyway I think Bobby and his family suffered enough."

I turned to Joey feeling ashamed and simply said, "Thank you."

Adam put his hand on Joey's shoulder and told him, "Joey, we will take care of you."

Maz then grabbed the other arm and both of them walked with him to the police car. Maz placed Joey in the back seat. Joey stared out the back window as the police car drove away.

I asked Adam, "What is going to happen to Joey now?"

Adam looked away. "I don't know, Bobby."

I knew there probably wasn't much he could do.

46

I couldn't believe what the newspaper article said. *Joey Bettino to plead guilty to the charge of murder in the first degree at his sentencing tomorrow.* That meant that Joey was going to get the death penalty. It had just been reinstated last year in New York State.

I called Maz. "Is this true about Joey, that he wants to plead guilty to murder? I know all the evidence points at him, but at least he could have pled down and served the rest of his life in prison."

Maz sighed heavily. "Yes, it is true, Bobby. I talked to Adam the other day. He even tried to talk him out of it, but you how stubborn Joey is. He says he can't take going back to the joint anymore and wants to leave the death penalty on the table."

I felt guiltier than ever. "Are you going to his sentencing tomorrow?" I asked Maz.

"I'll meet you at the courthouse, Bobby."

The Brooklyn Courthouse looked the same as it did thirty years ago. We sat in the front. There was no sign of Adam in the courtroom. Two court officers brought Joey in front of the judge. Joey winked at Maz and I. We all stood as the judge walked into the courtroom.

The judge spoke. "Joey Bettino, you have pleaded guilty to two counts of murder in the first degree. Have you anything to say to the court?"

"Yes, Your Honor. I have committed two inexcusable murders. I am willing to face the consequences."

"Mr. Bettino, that means that you will face the death penalty."

I was wondering why Adam was not here in behalf of Joey.

"Yes, Your Honor, I understand."

"Then so be it. You are sentenced to death by lethal injection."

Everyone in the courtroom started to whisper to each other. The judge smacked his gravel. "Order in the court, order in the court." Reporters got up and ran out of the courtroom to make the five o'clock edition. The judge said to the two court officers, "Take him away."

Joey looked down at the ground as the two court officers led him into another room.

Maz and I walked out of the courthouse. We stood out front for a while just trying to catch our breath. A news reporter came over to us to ask if we knew Joey and if we would like to say a few words on camera. Maz said, "No thanks." Then the reporter sarcastically told us, "This couldn't happen to a nicer guy." Maz then pushed the news reporter to the ground.

The reporter yelled, "You just assaulted me!"

I corrected the reporter. "Believe me, that wasn't an assault. This is an assault." Maz then lunged at me, holding me back from the reporter.

The reporter jumped up and ran away.

Maz looked at me. "I don't know if it's to late, but we have to visit Joey and try to talk him out of this. I'll call Adam to see if he wants to come. Bobby, I'll call you next week."

47

It seemed like old times again. There we were, going back to Greenville State Penitentiary. I met Maz at his home. Adam was going to meet us at Greenville. Maz drove. There was more traffic on the thruway than there was twenty years ago. More and more people were moving into the suburbs. If you don't mind an hour to an hour and a half commute, it is a great place to live.

I asked Maz, "When are you are retiring from the job?"

Maz started to laugh. "Tomorrow. No, I am seriously thinking about it. I have over twenty years. I could get a pension. The job is changing. They want you to do more with less. The big bosses have this new downtown meeting that they call Comstat. The meeting is held every month. Comstat is all about numbers and crime statistics. If a particular precinct's crime is up then the commanding officer is called to the meeting. They like to chew out their subordinates in front of their peers if they are not holding up their standards. Then my boss chews me out because he gets reprimanded. Everything rolls down hill.

I think it is a little immature to do it that way. But hey, that's my opinion."

I told Maz, "I am thinking of selling the business and retiring to Florida. I cannot compete with the bigger companies. Their prices are much lower compared to mine because they buy in such large quantities and have the room to store the merchandise."

Maz suggested with a smile, "Well, let's do it then."

We pulled into the Greenville parking lot. Adam was waiting for us in the main lobby. He told the guard that we were there to see Joey Bettino.

Adam walked over to us. "It's going to be a few minutes. Let's sit down."

I asked Adam, "Are you running for another term?"

"I'd like to, Bobby. I enjoy serving the people of this state."

"Spoken like a true politician," I said, and we both started laughing.

Maz turned to Adam and asked him seriously, "Is that why you're not doing anything to help Joey?"

Adam looked away from Maz in disgust. "I did ask the warden to look out for Joey. It wasn't the same asshole as before."

Maz smirked. "Big deal."

The guard came over and told us to follow him. It was the same smelly hallways; only the guards were different. The guard opened a door that led to a small room away from the normal visitors' room. I guess Adam did have some pull. Joey was standing by himself in the corner. There was no one else in the room except us. Joey looked terrible. It was hard to believe that he was skinnier than before. He also looked white as a ghost.

Adam was the first to speak. "Joey, how are they treating you in here?"

Joey sat back with a smirk on his face. "Oh, I can't complain," he said.

I felt obliged to say, "Joey, I'd like to thank you for what you did."

Maz interrupted. "Joey, Joey, Joey . . . why didn't you let me take care of it? We were so close to those shitheads. I wanted the satisfaction of bringing them in myself and watching them fry."

Joey wasn't saying much. A minute went by and no one spoke. Joey then sat down next to Adam. I couldn't believe the words that came out of his mouth. "Buddy, we have known each other for a long time. Can you do me one more favor? Can you get me out of here one more time? It could have been you waiting on death row instead of me."

We were all in shock. It was never like Joey to turn soft like that. Why did he plead guilty to murder? I guess I could understand -- it was his life he was talking about.

Adam put his arm around Joey's shoulder. "Buddy, there is something that I am working on. I am trying to pass a bill that would remove the death penalty from New York State law. It is going to take some time but I will get it done."

Like a little kid I yelled, "That is great, Adam!"

But Joey and Maz weren't excited. Maz sneered, "Yeah, that is great." Joey just sat in his chair and did not say a word.

We all hugged Joey good-bye. We walked through

the gates and into the parking lot. You could see the tears in Adam's eyes. I never saw him cry like that. We shook hands and said good-bye. Adam looked up to the sky and told Maz and I, "Let's pray for a person who is a greater man than us."

48

I t's been three years since I sold the store and my house on Staten Island and moved to Florida. I had a heart attack two years ago. It wasn't as severe as my father's but I was hospitalized for a week. Anne and I had a three-bedroom home built on the land that we purchased four years ago. Robert moved down with us. Jack remained in New York with his wife and two daughters. Barbara moved down with her husband and two children. They bought a home about five miles from us.

Maz is still a detective with the NYPD. He made first grade. He wants to stay a few more years to supplement his pension. I think Adam put in a good word for him with the police commissioner.

As for Adam, he never ran for re-election. The press gave him a hard time for being friends with Joey and previously granting his pardon, only to have Joey commit another murder. This time for real. However, Adam did play a big part in having the death penalty removed from the New York penal code. It took two years, but it was finally removed.

Joey now is facing two life sentences in Greenville

State Penitentiary. I gave up writing to him. I wrote a letter every month but he never responded.

As For me, I took up the sport of golf. I'd never touched a golf club in my life. I play with Robert almost every day. Now I can't put the clubs down.

Dedicated To

Constantine and Anne Paluszek